Practical Hexes

The Witches of Hollow Cove
Book Five

Kim Richardson

This book is a work of fiction. Any references to historical events, real people, or real locales are used fictitiously. Other names, characters, places, and incidents are the product of the author's imagination, and any resemblance to actual events, locales, or persons, living or dead, is entirely coincidental.

Practical Hexes, The Witches of Hollow Cove, Book Five
Copyright © 2021 by Kim Richardson
All rights reserved, including the right of reproduction
in whole or in any form.

www.kimrichardsonbooks.com

PRACTICAL HEXES

THE WITCHES OF HOLLOW COVE
BOOK FIVE

KIM RICHARDSON

1

Tonight, I was the Soul Collector's slave.

If you haven't been following my story, well, let me bring you up to speed.

A grieving father in Hollow Cove summoned the soul collector (a Greater demon from the Netherworld) to save his little girl's life in exchange for a whopping crapload of souls. It's no surprise the demon agreed.

That was where I came in.

To save all those souls—including my gran's—as well as the little girl's life, I offered the soul collector my services for a month.

In my haste, I'd agreed before I understood fully what it meant to be in the service of a demon. According to Marcus, I was the demon's *slave*.

Well, imagine the tsunami of theories that

popped into my head about what being a demon's slave entailed. And none of them were good.

Sex slave was the first thing that appeared in the forefront of my mind, and the idea of the soul collector's creepy, skeletal fingers touching my skin made me want to hurl. I had no idea what I was in for when I accepted.

Guess I was about to find out.

"Are you okay?"

I lifted my gaze at the worry in Marcus's voice. The chief had been by my side since the soul collector had practically jumped us from the shadows five minutes ago, just as we were about to climb up the steps to Davenport House's front porch. At the time, I was in Marcus's arms, hoping to get the *release* of the century.

Yeah, that didn't happen.

A frown creased those fine, gray eyes framed with dark eyelashes. It was still snowing, and big fat snowflakes peppered his tussled black hair. It took some serious self-control to not roll my face in it. His high cheekbones were colored with anger, which only made him sexier. Cauldron help me, he was beautiful.

He stood on the front porch next to me, all confident and predatory with his arms crossed over his ample chest, making his broad shoulders stand out and his pecs bulge. He was a virile beast, a muscle machine who was just as strong as he was a tender lover.

I cursed on the inside.

I only regretted that I wasn't going to get my Fifty Shades of Marcus tonight. And that, ladies, put me in a foul mood.

Especially since everything had been cleared up with Allison—a.k.a. Marcus's gorgeous ex. I deserved a little release!

"I feel like my innards went to a barn dance," I answered finally.

The chief made a sound in his throat that seemed very close to a growl. Marcus shifted his weight, his gaze flicking from me to the soul collector who waited just beyond the stone path. The chief seemed to be contemplating whether or not to take down the demon.

Marcus was strong and fierce. In his beast form, he could tear apart the greatest of adversaries, but the soul collector was a Greater demon. I seriously doubted the wereape's strength would make the slightest difference against him. If my aunts couldn't defeat him, neither could Marcus.

But none of that mattered. I'd made a deal with the demon, and I had to make good on it if I didn't want my gran's soul and all the other souls to return to the in-between only to be traded to other demons to be ingested or tortured.

My gaze settled on the soul collector. His white eyes and hairless face were partially covered by his black fedora. With his thin, gangly limbs, he looked like a scarecrow in a dark suit, his movements stiff and disjointed like he was a stop-motion character.

His briefcase hanging from his right hand, the soul collector rocked back and forth on the balls of his feet, just a few paces away from the stone path (which was covered in snow at the moment) directly off the property line. I'd noticed he was very careful to stand on the outskirts of the Davenport House's property.

Once I realized the soul collector wasn't a figment of my imagination and wasn't going to go away, I'd excused myself. My bladder was about to explode as I made my way to the small powder room to the right of the entryway to relieve myself. When I came back, I found the soul collector waiting for me in the exact same spot.

For some reason, the demon wouldn't or couldn't enter the property. I was betting on the *couldn't*. Perhaps Davenport House's magic prohibited him from entering.

That was interesting indeed. I was going to save that valuable piece of information for later and do some digging.

The demon pulled out an old-fashioned pocket watch from his jacket. He glanced at it and said,

"Time to go, Tessa Davenport," in a voice just as banal and pedestrian as his suit before he slipped the watch back into the folds of his jacket. If he'd had a harsh, guttural kind of voice, well, at least it would have been a bit more interesting.

My heart slammed in my chest. "Where are we going?" I shot a nervous glance at Marcus before climbing down the porch's steps and joining the soul collector with the chief following closely behind me.

"You'll find out soon enough," answered the demon. His hairless brows rose and disappeared under his hat. "I almost forgot." He dropped his briefcase on the ground, opened it, and pulled out a pile of folded clothes. "Here," he said and shoved the clothes at me. "Your uniform."

I choked on my spit. "My what?"

"Your uniform," the demon added brightly. "Go on. Take it."

My curiosity getting the better of me, I took the pile of clothes and went through them. A white shirt, a pair of dark slacks, and matching a jacket. And... wait for it—a tie.

"It's a suit. A man's suit." I wrinkled my brow. "Is this *your* suit?" Gross. The idea of wearing one of the soul collector's suits made me gag. The night was getting weirder by the minute.

The soul collector reached down and grabbed his briefcase, shutting it with a loud snap. "It's not mine. It's yours. It was made especially for you. Now, put it on and make haste. We have lots of work to do tonight."

I don't know what possessed me, but I drew the pile of clothes to my face and sniffed. "It smells like it came from a thrift shop from the 1980s." Making a face, I held the clothes out to the demon. "Forget it. I'm not wearing that." Okay, so I might be his slave, but I wasn't going to make it easy for him.

"It has been washed," noted the demon, irritation thick in his voice.

"With what? Mothballs and crud?" I brought the clothes closer to my face again. "Look. See that? I just saw a flea jump off. I don't do fleas."

The skin of the demon's face stretched tightly over muscle and bone, his expression stiff with frustration. "You are being ridiculous."

"It's called hygiene."

The demon's white eyes pinched with anger. "You are in *my* service, and those in *my* service wear a uniform. Put on the damn uniform!"

Netherworld be damned. "Fine." I let out a breath and gestured with my free hand. "Turn around."

The demon looked surprised. "Excuse me?"

I pressed a hand on my hip. "You heard me. Turn around so I can change." I did realize it was winter, but I was boiling with so much anger and adrenaline, I doubted I'd feel the cold.

Doing as instructed, the soul collector turned his back to me. It was all I could do not to kick him in the ass right now. That might even make wearing the mothball stinking suit worth the while. Maybe not.

"I can't believe I'm doing this," I huffed in frustration as I stripped out of my clothes down to my black bra and underwear.

I wasn't even embarrassed at being half-naked outside in the middle of winter. My new lady balls were making me brash.

My eyes found Marcus, and my throat tightened at the pain and frustration written all over his face. His gray eyes held a mixture of anguish and worry as he lifted them to me.

"Not exactly how you'd envisioned seeing me in my underwear for the second time, huh?" I said, trying to lighten the mood. It didn't work.

A whisper of cool air rolled off my skin, but I barely noticed. All my attention was on the mothball-stinking suit I had to pull over my clean skin.

"I should get paid for this crap." Making a face, I grabbed the pants, slipped my feet through the legs, and hauled them up. Next, holding my breath, I pulled on the white shirt and slid the jacket over it. Though they still had that nasty, years-in-your-great-aunt's-closet smell, they fit. Like perfectly. As though the suit was tailored to me.

"What is this?" I ran my hands over the fabric, trying to determine what it was. It felt and looked like rayon, but it was more durable and subtle, unlike any fabric I'd ever seen or touched before. My fingers tingled with cold energy.

Magic. Demon magic.

"Is something wrong?" asked Marcus, leaning next to me with his hands to his sides. He looked like he was ready to rip off my new outfit, which at another time and place would have been totally acceptable—more than acceptable.

I shook my head. "They fit," I told him, seeing the soul collector spin back around. "How did you know my size?" I demanded, remembering that he'd mentioned the clothes were made especially for me.

A satisfied smile blossomed over the demon's face. "It's on your ticket."

I rolled my eyes. "I'm going to make you eat that ticket."

"You're missing the tie," said the demon, as though I hadn't spoken. "You must look the part. It doesn't work without it. We mustn't forget the tie."

I picked the tie up from the snow. "If there's a hat involved... I might have to kill you."

The soul collector frowned. "Put on the tie."

I screwed up my face. "I have no idea how to do

this," I said, holding out the plain black tie. "I'm a female, remember? But... if you want a flawless cat-eye while driving—I'm your woman."

"Here. Let me do it." Marcus took the tie from me and draped it over my head, tugging me closer. He leaned forward, his chest rubbing against my breasts. His fingertips brushed against my jaw and neck. Fire erupted in my core, and my heart pounded. I took in the smell of man, soap, and something musky. I wanted to make love to that smell.

Marcus adjusted my tie and stepped back. I immediately felt the loss of his heat.

I stared down at my uniform. "I feel like one of the characters in the movie *Men in Black*." I felt like an idiot. Still, my annoyance about the clothes was keeping me from a major freak-out concerning what I was about to do. About to become.

"Come along now, Tessa Davenport," urged the demon. "Souls are waiting to be... *collected*."

I didn't like the sound of that, but it was a hell of a lot better than being a demon sex slave.

I blew out a nervous breath, scooped up my clothes off the ground, and handed them to Marcus. The fear on his beautiful face nearly did me in. "Don't tell my aunts or my mum," I said, my voice hoarse like it was lodged somewhere in my throat and didn't want to come out. "I'll tell them when I get back." I forced a laugh. "They're probably still drunk, anyway. Right?" I recalled their binge drinking in sorrow fest because they thought I'd died earlier tonight.

A muscle pulled on Marcus's jaw. "Be safe," he said, crushing my clothes against his chest. "I'll see you when you get back."

I tried to answer, but my jaw wouldn't unhinge, so I just nodded.

Emotions flickered through his eyes. I recognized fear, loss, and protectiveness in the mix. I knew he could sense my fear, and all he wanted to do was protect me and make me feel safe. Now he was helpless to do so, and it was tearing him apart.

But I'd gotten myself into this mess, and it was up to me to figure it out.

Then Marcus did something that surprised me.

He pressed his hands on my shoulders, leaned in, dipped his head, and kissed me.

My heart nearly exploded with emotions at the softness of his kiss as our mouths parted. It was fast but enough for me to feel the intent behind it—the breathless fear of not knowing what was going to happen.

"For luck," said Marcus as he pulled away. "You're going to need it." A brief look of pain passed over his features.

"I know." Regrettably, I forced myself to move

away from Marcus, though every muscle in my body begged me to stay.

But I had no choice. I was about to embark on one of the stupidest things I'd ever done. And I'd done my share of stupid. This scared the crap out of me.

Holding my breath, I stepped next to the soul collector and then everything around me vanished.

2

What does a witch do when she's traveling interdimensionally?

She screams. She screams *a lot*.

Still, I had some experience with otherworldly traveling from ley lines and having been literally swallowed into a demon's briefcase. So, my freak-out only lasted a few moments, but it was full-blown either way.

Darkness swathed me. It didn't matter if I had my eyes open or not. It was all the same. I saw nothing but a deep, endless blackness as I drifted to wherever I was supposed to go.

Speaking of said otherworldly traveling, it had the same pulling effects I'd experienced with the soul collector's briefcase trip—only without the pain.

Trust me, I would have howled like the banshee of the universe if it had been painful. It occurred to me I should have felt pain, lots and lots of it, but something or someone had made sure I didn't feel it.

And then it hit me.

The suit. The suit the soul collector forced me to wear protected me from having my body blasted into millions of chunks while world-jumping. I had no idea what else to call it. Without the suit, I'd be soup-Tessa.

The pulling stopped as my feet hit solid ground. Breathing hard with my gaze unfocused, I felt vertigo take over. Thank the cauldron I didn't have much food in me. Otherwise, I would have been sick right about now.

The darkness around me lifted until I could make out walls and furniture. I was in someone's house.

When the dizziness passed, I looked around properly. The house itself was elegant—spacious with high ceilings, floor-to-ceiling windows, and polished wide wood plank floors that were rare these days. All the doorways stood in graceful wooden frames, and the walls were covered in art. Only a few sconces on the walls lit the space, creating deep pools of shadow where the corridors ended.

Where Davenport House was cozy and unpretentious, this place was snobbish with a stuffy museum-like feel, like you were only allowed to look but not touch. It wasn't my kind of place. I was in a mansion. That part was obvious.

"Come along now, Tessa Davenport." With his briefcase swinging in his hand, the soul collector waltzed down an enormous hallway decorated with paintings that probably cost more than the average car.

We passed a large library, its walls lined with old books in leather bindings. Leather-cushioned chairs had been placed in corners to provide private reading sessions.

I hurried after him, my boots stepping over Asian rugs, and I winced internally at the grime I was leaving on them. I had a weakness for rugs—and really most things I couldn't afford.

"What's your name? If we're going to work together, I should know what to call you. Unless you want me to keep calling you SC?" I knew if the demon gave me his real name, I could use it against him for things like spelling his skinny ass back to the Netherworld for good. It was also why I suspected my father, my demon father, went by the name Obi-Wan Kenobi.

"So... SC, it is, then." I figured if I was to be in his presence for a month, we might as well be on a first-name basis.

"Don't call me that," snapped the soul collector demon.

"I can't make that promise."

Not bothering to turn around, he announced, "You can call me Captain Jack Sparrow."

I felt my brows reach the bridge of my nose, also known as the WTF frown. "Do all demons give themselves fictitious movie character names?" What was up with that?

Okay. So, he did have a way of moving his legs like he was on a deck at sea, which could be interpreted as Captain Jack Sparrow-esque, but he was no Jonny Depp.

No answer. Guess he wasn't that stupid after all, but I wasn't about to give up. I would discover his real name. Because his real name was *my* ticket out of this nightmare. If I knew a demon's name, I had control over him.

"Okay, then. Jack, it is." I trudged along behind him, my eyes wide as I tried to take in everything around me, like exits in case I needed a quick getaway.

Even though the walls and floors were decorated with great beauty, we were about to do something ugly and nasty. I wasn't a hundred percent sure, but it didn't take a genius to figure out that when things involved a soul collector, they weren't all sunshine and rainbows. Not after seeing little Margorie.

Only desperate people made deals with demons. And at any second, I was about to find out just how desperate.

My heart thundered in my ears as I tried to keep my wits about me. Freaking out now wouldn't look good on my first day in front of my new boss—my new demon boss. A shiver lifted through me. I hadn't known the depth of my stupidity when I'd offered my services to him. All I could think about was Gran and the other undead. Marcus was right. I was impulsive, and one day it would get me killed.

I had to keep reminding myself that I was only doing this to keep my side of the deal. I wanted to keep Gran's and all those other souls safe. Besides, it was only one month. I could do this. I *had* to do this. I had no other choice.

Jack slipped through one of the many doors, and I followed him in.

It was a bedroom the size of Davenport House's first floor and large enough to make you wince and worry whether you'd make it to the bathroom on time in the middle of the night. I'd never been in a bedroom this size, and it made me wonder why people felt the need to make them this big unless they wanted to fit all of the von Trapp children.

The furniture was just as large and pompous as the room. In old Victorian style, the bulky pieces were carved from rich hardwoods in intricate designs, gleaming in the yellow light.

In the middle of the room rested a bed that could have fit an elephant comfortably. A wizened man lay there with his head propped up on a pile of pillows, and his eyes frowned at our approach. He looked like a caricature of a man carved from dried tree roots. If he'd had hair once, it was long gone now. He was bald, just like the soul collector.

Jack approached the bed, rocking his briefcase like it was payday. Guess it was.

"Xander McCormack. I'm here to collect." Jack smiled, a creepy, selfie kind of smile like he was posing for a few seconds to get the shot. His white eyes widened, and I could see the black of his pupils for the first time.

I felt ill, knowing he was about to get this poor man's soul. Though the man did look like he'd seen his one-hundredth birthday a while ago, it was still disturbing.

Xander's lips moved for a few beats until words wheezed out. "Not. Yet."

Jack lowered his briefcase onto the bed next to the old man. "The deal was... I'd make you rich until your last breath." The soul collector pulled out his pocket watch. "Which is in precisely... sixty-three seconds."

I tensed as Xander began to hack wet, sickly

coughs, the kind that came from someone who'd been a heavy smoker longer than I'd been alive.

"I'm not dead yet," wheezed Xander. His eyes moved over to me, and I flinched at the hate I saw in them. Of course, he thought I was a demon too, a soul collector. Guess I was.

"He's human." It wasn't a question. I could tell the old man was human. One clue was that he wasn't giving off any of the familiar paranormal energies.

Jack turned to look at me. "Does that surprise you? Humans are seventy percent of my clientele. They're greedy. Fame and fortune seekers. And lazy. Most of the time they opt for the easy route, which is when they find me."

"I wouldn't call it easy, but I am surprised humans are aware of you." Truthfully, I'd always assumed all the souls were paranormal, not human souls. Apparently, I still had a lot to learn, even about my own paranormal world.

Looking around, the man was stinking rich, and he likely hadn't worked for any of it. It was kind of like finding a jinni and making a wish, but there was a catch. Your soul belonged to the soul collector... in perpetuity.

Xander's pale and clammy face paled even more. "Monsters," he managed. "Devils."

Yup. He was referring to us.

"I'm not dying today," said the old man. He

moved his arms like he was trying to push himself up but couldn't.

Jack flashed him a smile that would have had grown men scattering away like frightened rodents before a cat. "Oh yes. I can assure you that you are dying tonight, my friend. Just like we planned it all those years ago."

"Does he know what's going to happen to his soul? Does he know all the details? The fine print?" I moved closer to the bed on the demon's right side so I had a better view and also because I could barely hear the old man.

I felt my underwear rise into my butt crack. My new suit seemed to pull on my cotton undies. Inconspicuously, I shifted my weight from leg to leg, trying to dislodge the culprit, but it didn't work. The only thing it did was make me look like I had an itch. So, I did the only thing I could.

I dug in there and pulled it out.

"What are you doing?" Jack's face was an array of expressions I didn't think he was capable of showing.

"Nothing." Oops. Heat rushed to my face. Not so inconspicuous after all. At least I'd taken care of the wedgie.

Jack stared at me for a beat longer. "He knows, but he wanted to be rich."

"I *am* rich," coughed Xander, like that meant

anything now. Looks like it meant a great deal to him. Even on his death bed, he felt the need to proclaim his wealth. I felt sorry for him, even if he kept giving me his "angry eyes." Not because of his lost soul, though that did come a close second, but because in his mind he felt as though being rich, having all these material things, somehow made him special. It didn't.

Jack glimpsed at his pocket watch. "Shall we do the countdown together?"

My face fell in shock. "What? No." The demon was sick. I didn't want to take part in that, but I wasn't sure I had a choice. Apparently, I did since Jack didn't insist. Thank the cauldron for that. I took a step back for good measure. Also, because I knew what was about to happen.

"Five," counted Jack, his voice cheery and rising in tempo like a gameshow host.

My face went cold, and I felt my stomach drop.

"Four."

"You can't take my soul," hissed Xander, clearly not ready to give up all of his precious belongings. "I'm going to live on. I'm in perfect health. You'll see. I'm fine."

"Three."

"I'm the richest man in Florida," he continued, "and the most powerful." Huh. I had no idea we'd skipped a few states. If I wasn't so disgusted and freaked out, I might have been impressed at the soul collector's means of traveling.

"Two."

"I'm not dying. I feel fine." Xander's face was as white as his sheets. "You're wrong."

"One."

Xander opened his mouth, smiled, and said. "See? I told you—"

His head shook in quick, jerky spasms as his eyes widened. He cried out, but I wasn't sure if it was from agony or fear. His body tightened, muscles convulsing just as they would on an electrocuted human being. And then his eyes went dull, stopped like a clock, just as I heard his last breath escape from his lips.

"Ah. There we are. Excellent. Just excellent." Jack slipped his pocket watch inside his jacket and placed his hands on his hips, waiting.

In a sudden burst of brilliant light, Xander's body glittered, like his skin was made up of millions of sparkling jewels. I flinched. I didn't know why. I'd seen this before.

The brilliant jewels over his skin then detached themselves and drifted above his body, slowly coming together in a ball of light.

And then the ball of light zoomed into the briefcase and disappeared.

Jack snapped the briefcase shut. "And that's how

it's done," the demon complimented himself. He smiled like his boss had just given him a big fat raise.

My eyes found Xander again. It was just like the other times I'd seen the souls leave their bodies. Except that Xander wasn't an undead, and his body hadn't combusted into ash.

I shuddered at the panic I'd seen in his eyes in that split second before he died. I'd seen the fear in his eyes, the regret, and it was the most disturbing thing I'd ever witnessed. I never wanted to see it again—ever—but I knew I would.

Jack moved past me and stood in the middle of the room, his briefcase clasped in his hand. "Well, I think this exercise was extremely beneficial as part of your basic education in soul collecting. It could not have gone any better if I'd done it alone. Questions?"

"No."

"Excellent. Well then. You're done for the night."

"Thank the cauldron," I muttered, feeling relieved. If being his slave meant I only had to witness and not do the actual taking of the soul, I could live with that. I guessed my month wasn't going to be that bad after all.

Feeling marginally better, I moved over to stand next to Jack.

The demon glanced at his pocket watch again before slipping it inside his jacket. "We've made excellent time. I have a few things to take care of before the night is over, but I'll take you home now. Come along, Tessa Davenport."

I sighed. "Great." I'd only just realized how tired I was. The idea of seeing my bed again had me all tingly inside. Too bad there wasn't a wereape in it.

"Now that you've been acquainted with the process," continued Jack, "it'll be *your* turn tomorrow night."

"Excuse me?" I felt my stomach twist and fall somewhere between my feet on the expensive Persian rug.

"Janet Purcell's soul is next on my list," answered the demon. "And you... are going to get it for me."

Yeah, my world just got a hell of a lot more complicated.

3

I woke to a pounding headache, the kind where even your teeth hurt. I looked around my room, the effort making my eyeballs sting. My throat burned, and when I swallowed, even my ears hurt. That was new.

Moaning, I propped myself on my elbows, my muscles screaming. Every cell in my body hurt. Hell, everything hurt. I felt like the time I'd spent four hours in the gym training on every machine available without having a clue as to how to operate them.

I winced as I moved my head to look around my room. Thankfully, it was still just as large and breathtaking. House had kept it looking like the master bedroom of my dreams.

The only thing missing was a gray-eyed, sexy as

sin wereape naked in my bed. Naked with me naked next to him, in my bed.

But a tall, gorgeous blonde crept into my happy thoughts, and my mood soured like a bad fruit. Allison. She wasn't going to give Marcus up easily. She was a fighter, that one. But guess what? I was too.

Still, waking up to a room that was perfectly me did feel awesome. Gran had been the one to tell me about Davenport House's magical room enlargement capability. I felt a pang in my chest at the thought of that little old witch. I was going to miss her.

My aches and pains were no doubt a result of world-jumping with Captain Jack Sparrow. As a mortal, and only part demon, my body wasn't used to or formulated for that kind of supernatural travel. Ley lines were different. They were magical. And as a magical being, I could manipulate them, though not all witches could.

That was where the suit Jack had fitted me with came to play. It kept me alive and made world-jumping, demon style, possible.

Yet I couldn't shake off the feeling that even with the suit, if I wasn't half-demon, I didn't think it would have been possible.

Jack knew who my father was. Was this why he'd been so happy to oblige my end of the deal? Yeah. I bet it was.

Speaking of said suit, I spotted the dark pant suit

draped over my chair, where I'd left it last night. It hadn't combusted into flame or crumbled into dust as I slept. The damn thing looked perfect like it had just come back from the dry cleaners, all ironed and ready to wear.

I sat up, winced in pain, and reached out to grab my phone from my night table. I had a new text from Marcus.

Text me when you wake up.

I texted him back.

I'm up. I feel fine. Don't worry.

I knew he was worried. I wasn't going to lie. It felt damn good to know he was worried about me. I swiped the screen, re-reading his texts from last night. The chief had been a mess if his short, mashed-up text messages were an indicator. Knowing what I knew about him, he'd probably been out of his mind with worry until I got back.

Good thing he was the first person I'd texted when I was home.

I'm fine, I'd texted him.

I was too tired to call, and I knew my voice would betray me because I wasn't fine at all. Quite the opposite.

I knew Marcus was busying himself imagining the worst, things that were not even worth thinking about without making me cringe. I'd texted him the truth, that it had been more of an orientation kind of night. I had only observed. The soul collector only wanted me as his audience, or some crap like that.

I hadn't mentioned what I was going to do tonight, though.

The thought made my stomach churn and my head throb even more. Tonight, *I* was going to retrieve Janet Purcell's soul. Would Jack give me a briefcase? Would Janet die from old age like Xander? And all I had to do was just stand there and do nothing? I hoped so, and even that thought alone made me sick.

Xander had regretted it, but only when he knew he was dying, and his soul was Jack's. I'd seen it—the fear and the regret. Guess being the richest man in Florida meant nothing if your soul belonged to the devil.

What happened if I didn't get the soul? What if I decided I didn't want to? Would the soul be safe? Would Jack take my soul instead? No. He would take Gran's and all the other souls.

It seemed I had a lot to learn, but I still had all day to prepare for that. Mentally. The physical part I could live with, but the mental part frightened me— the horrors of what I was going to be part of and what I would be forced to do.

At that moment, my stomach gave a loud growl. When I glanced at the clock on my phone, I knew why I was so hungry. It was lunchtime.

After brushing my teeth and taking a hot shower, I got dressed in casual jeans and a black sweater and went downstairs. Following the smell of coffee, I stepped into the kitchen and burst out laughing. Then I regretted it as my temples throbbed like I had miniature jackhammers occupying the space between my skull and skin.

Dolores looked up from the kitchen table and glared at me. She had bags under her eyes, but they were still calculating, assessing. "What's so funny?" Her voice was harsh and low like she'd used crushed glass as a mouthwash.

Beverly sat across from Dolores, a coffee mug wrapped in her red-manicured fingers. She had a knot the size of my fist in the back of her blonde hair. It was a mess, and she had a mudslide of yesterday's mascara dried to her cheeks.

Ruth, well, she had her eyes closed and was slowly moving her body in circles on her seat, her arms out like she was trying to maintain her balance while walking a tightrope. I wasn't surprised to find that she wasn't busy with lunch. She looked like she might puke lunch. However, an unopened bag of bagels sat in the middle of the table with my name on it.

"You look like me, back in college after my first hangover. Like your liver is failing." I tried to keep the laughter from my voice but failed miserably.

They looked worse than me. Much worse. And in some sick way, it made me feel better. Iris had texted me from Ronin's last night, so I didn't expect to see her here.

To my surprise, the kitchen was clean, the evidence of my aunts' vodka and wine binge gone. House had probably taken care of that for them, no doubt. Living in a magical home had its perks and then some.

After I'd poured myself a steaming cup of coffee, I pulled out the chair next to Beverly and let myself fall into it. "They say the best way to cure a hangover... is to have another drink."

Beverly turned and gave me an ice-cold stare. "Do you want to die?"

I shrugged. "I'm just saying. I've never actually tried it, but it might help. Maybe Ruth has a hangover remedy she can fix you up with?" When my eyes found Ruth, her lips were pressed tightly together, and she looked green. "Maybe not."

Dolores dropped her coffee mug on the table with a loud thud. "We look like this because we thought you were dead. That's why. Ow." She rubbed her forehead with her fingertips. "See what you made us do?"

"Next time don't mix vodka and wine," I offered and bit the inside of my cheek at Beverly's glare so I wouldn't start laughing. "And drink water. Lots and lots of water."

Dolores gestured with her right hand over the table. "Give me the Tylenol. My brain is trying to break through my skull."

I leaned forward and snatched up the bottle of Tylenol from the wicker basket to give to her. "Is my mum in her room?" I asked as I sat back down and took a sip of my coffee, letting the bitter and sweet aroma roll over my tongue before swallowing.

The aunts shared a look, except for Ruth whose eyes were still shut.

"What?" I stared at them, waiting. Something was up. They looked guilty.

Dolores popped two Tylenol into her mouth, downed them with some coffee, and said, "She's gone. She left early this morning after speaking to Sean. I'm sorry, Tessa. I'm sorry she left without saying goodbye."

"Don't be," I told them, and I really meant it. "I'm used to it. Besides, this life, this magical life, was never her. She belongs with him, the person who makes her happy." The truth was, she'd been found out. My father was a demon, and she didn't want to be here when I confronted her.

She was a coward, which didn't surprise me.

My stomach grumbled and I shot to my feet. "Well, after the night I had, I need carbs. Lots and lots of delicious carbs." I grabbed the bag of bagels from the table, snatched one out, and stuck it in the toaster oven.

Beverly ran a finger lightly over the pearls around her neck. "I don't think I could eat anything, if I'd died and came back," she said, staring at the bag of bagels like it contained maggots.

That's not what I'd meant. I was referring to my work with the soul collector. They still had no idea what kind of night I'd had, and I knew I couldn't keep this from them.

"How are we supposed to defeat the soul collector when our livers are in withdrawal?" asked Dolores, her face drawn and pale.

"Um. About that." I waited until I had their full attention, which were the frowns from Dolores and Beverly with Ruth grimacing but not opening her eyes.

I cleared my voice and said, "The soul collector is gone. The souls are safe. Gran is safe. They're all safe."

Dolores eyed me for a long moment. "How?" And then, seeing something on my face she added, "What did you do, Tessa?"

So, I told them everything that had happened, even the repeated part of my spending time in the in-between with Gran since when I told them last night they'd all been too inebriated to make any sense of it. I explained about my father being a demon, to the very last detail of me making a deal with the soul collector.

When I was done, I crossed my arms over my chest, waiting for the information to sink in and for the aftermath of the shitshow to follow.

Silence soaked the room, broken only by the ding of the toaster oven, proclaiming my bagel was ready. I didn't dare move.

Dolores's right eye started to twitch like she had a spasm or something. Either that or she was about to have a brain aneurysm. "You made a deal with a demon? A soul collector?" Her voice was strangely high and quavering, very unlike herself.

I swallowed hard. "I did. I did what I had to do. It was the only way to keep all the souls safe."

"I think I'm going to be sick." Ruth stumbled off her chair and ran out of the kitchen in a zigzag formation down the hall, her bare feet slapping the hardwood floors. I heard the door to the powder room slam shut.

Beverly settled back in her chair, a pinched expression creasing her pretty features. "Do you have to perform any sexual favors?" She actually looked interested, which was truly disturbing.

My mouth fell open. "Uhh... no... nothing like that. I just work with him."

"By taking mortal souls," expressed Dolores, her

voice gravely bitter. "Like your Gran's?" That revelation made Beverly gasp.

This was going so well I nearly broke into song. "Well, not exactly. I mean... kind of, I guess. I'm kind of like an assistant." *I think?*

Beverly threw her hands up in the air. "Cauldron help us. We are cursed. A Merlin in our family in the service of a demon. Who's ever heard of such a thing?"

"No one," answered Dolores, "because most Merlins know better than to bargain with demons." Her eyebrows rose high as she glared at me. "Rookie mistake."

Okay, now I was pissed. "Listen. It wasn't all that bad. The souls are under contract." I couldn't believe I was defending the soul collector. "These people knew what they were doing when they signed off their souls." Truthfully, I wasn't entirely sure that was the case. Jack could have just as easily tricked a large number of desperate humans and paranormals for their souls. Yeah. I was sure he had.

"So, you just... observe?" asked Dolores. "That's all you do? You don't hurt anyone? You just watch from the sidelines while he extracts souls?"

Here it comes. "Last night was just like an orientation. And yes. All I did was watch while he... well..."

"Took someone's soul," finished Dolores. "I can't

believe what I'm hearing. My own niece working for a demon."

"That's a bit much," I growled. "I am doing this to save all the other souls. Not to mention your mum's. You're acting like I *want* to do this. I don't. I *have* to. There's a difference."

Dolores's dark eyes met mine. "And all you have to do is watch, for an entire month? That doesn't seem profitable for the demon. Unless he enjoys having an audience while he rips the souls out of people."

He didn't rip them out, but I wasn't about to correct her. I nodded and said, "Jack says I've got to retrieve a soul later tonight." My insides quivered at the thought. I was not looking forward to that.

"Jack? Who's Jack?" asked Beverly, looking mildly interested at the mention of a male's name.

"The soul collector. He calls himself Captain Jack Sparrow," I said with a laugh, but I sobered up at the look of utter horror on Beverly's face.

She pushed back her chair and stood slowly, holding her head with both hands like it might fall off. "I don't feel well. I need to lie down." She left the kitchen without another word.

"I think this is all I can take of this new development as well. I need a nap," said Dolores pushing to her feet, the Tylenol bottle in her hand.

"Hey," I protested. "I thought you were going to

help me out with this? You're the ones with all the experience. I'm in need of experience."

Dolores gave me a tired look. "Experiences shape your brain. And right now, mine is all worn out. It needs to rest. And recharge." And with that, she too left the kitchen.

In a matter of minutes, it was just me and my bagel. How did that happen?

"Thanks for your help," I called out to them, not sure if they were listening or not. "But don't you worry about me. I can take care of myself. I'll be just fine."

But the truth was, I wasn't fine. Not by a long shot.

4

Since I had practically ten hours until my "night job," I figured I'd go see Marcus and give him a detailed account of my first night as Jack's slave. I knew he was worried, and knowing he cared sent little tingles of delight through my body.

I wasn't going to lie. Having the chief worry about me felt good, really good.

Yet, I still had to reassure him that I was fine and could handle this new gig. Hopefully. Maybe I'd try to reassure myself in the process.

With that in mind, and a new spring in my step, I walked along Stardust Drive, breathing in the cold, delightfully fresh air. I squinted in the afternoon glare, my thoughts moving from Marcus to my mother. If I didn't know any better, I'd say she'd acted like a sixteen-year-old girl who ran away from home because her parents forbade her from dating the high school star football player.

A bell sounded from my phone, pulling my thoughts from my mother. Thinking it was Marcus again, I reached into my bag and yanked it out. My eyebrows rose to my hairline. It was from Iris.

Iris: *You're welcome.*

I made a face. "You are one strange witch, Iris," I told my phone. "Even if I am talking to myself, you're still the weirder one." Laughing, I dropped my phone back into my bag. Maybe the text had been meant for Ronin after they'd spent the night together. Maybe he had *lots* to be thankful for.

Crossing Shifter Lane at a stroll, I hit the sidewalk and made a beeline to the Hollow Cove Security Agency building.

The clatter of a glass door opening was my only warning.

I yelped and lurched back just as Allison came rushing through, nearly smashing the door into my face.

I slipped on the wet snow but caught myself before I went sprawling on the sidewalk. Annoyance flared through me. I opened my mouth to tell her off, but one look at her face and the words on my tongue just vanished.

I'd always thought Allison's face put all of us women to shame, with her thick lashes, full red lips, large blue eyes, perfect luscious blonde hair, and voluptuous body that was every man's dream. She was drop-dead gorgeous—literally. An overweight man with high cholesterol could have a heart attack just looking at her. She probably looked like she just stepped off the catwalk when she woke up in the morning.

But now... now her face... holy hell. The skin on her face and her throat was covered in blotches of dark, angry red. Some had white heads. Some didn't.

Allison looked murderous at the sight of me. "You," she seethed, spit flying from the corners of her mouth, her eyes round and full of hate. "You did this! You did this to me! To me!" she added, as though I didn't catch that she was referring to herself.

Oh, dear. Now Iris's text started to make a lot of sense.

I tried not to smile, but my mouth seemed to have other plans. "Is that chicken pox or a bad case of acne?"

She stood with her back rigid, the fists at her sides trembling with barely controlled anger. She looked like she was about to go all gorilla Barbie on me. Instead, she took her blue wool scarf that matched her eyes and wrapped it around her head and neck until it looked like a niqab.

"You'll pay for this," she threatened, and I imagined she had a snarl on her lips under the scarf.

I thought about telling her I had nothing to do with her instant-acne, shingles, chicken pox, whatever, but I didn't want to get Iris into any trouble with the wereape. Iris had done this for me. Only a true friend would come up with such an extraordinarily ugly curse for the "other woman."

And I didn't feel sorry for Allison either. Not even a tiny bit.

A growl escaped her as she moved past me and disappeared inside her white Range Rover. I heard her SUV pull away from the curb just as the door to the chief's building closed behind me.

I smiled. This was going to be a great day.

I made my way inside, blinking into the harsh white lights. As I crossed the lobby, I was expecting the delightful scent of freshly brewed coffee, but I was hit instead by a wall of rotten meat stench, bleach, and something like cat pee.

The desks and chairs were pushed up against the walls, and a person in a white hazmat suit was sweeping a wet mop like they were trying to sand down the tile floor with it. I recognized the older woman with the short white hair and pinched expression behind the transparent plastic face visor.

"Hi, Grace," I said, my eyes watering at the powerful bleach smell, as I approached slowly. I swept my gaze across the floor, and my eyes settled on dark maroon spots that still held tiny bits of what looked to be strings of meat along with brown and honey puddles. That was not chocolate or caramel. More like some of the undeads' liquified leftovers.

Unlike Davenport House, which, no surprise, had magically removed all traces of the undead without me having lifted a finger by the time I went to inspect after my coffee. But Grace was not so lucky.

"Do you need some help?" The thought of the older woman doing all the work didn't settle well with me. Why were women always stuck cleaning?

"You step on my clean floor and I'll make you drink the bucket!" she growled, pointing with her mop to a shiny and very clean with no undead parts section of the floor.

Okay. Maybe not. "I wouldn't dream of it." I backed away carefully and slipped past Grace's scowl to make my way toward Marcus's office.

I edged toward the door with the name MARCUS DURAND stenciled on the window in black letters, the words CHIEF OFFICER written under it. Voices reached me as I approached. One, in particular, rose in pitch behind the closed door, and I'd recognize that shrill anywhere.

"Tessa Davenport should be fired!" the piercing voice hissed.

The door was shut, but since *I* was the subject of this heated discussion, I figured I should be there.

Grinding my teeth, I pushed in.

Marcus's office looked exactly like I remembered it. To the right of the door was a wall lined with filing cabinets, and rows of bookcases occupied the wall next to the desk. A single desk sat in front of the only window in the place, stacked with papers next to a laptop.

A broad-shouldered man with a tussle of black hair framing his chiseled jaw and a perfectly straight nose sat behind the desk. His long-sleeved black T-shirt did nothing to conceal his large chest or his flat stomach. He looked up, his intense gray eyes pinning me. My stomach erupted in delightful batting butterflies. I could get used to that.

I stood in the middle of the office, my hands on my hips, and said, "I should be fired? Really? For what?"

"Don't you knock? This is a private conversation," said a short, pudgy man with gray hair wearing a bow tie and epic frown. "Get out." He pointed to the door behind me like he was the boss of me.

Of course, that made me want to stay even more.

"I think I'll stay. If you're talking about me, I want to know about it, Gilbert."

Gilbert pulled his face into a sour expression, his

brown eyes full of rage. "Merlin or not. You're not entitled to *private* conversations."

"When they're about me, yes. And you can't fire me." I wasn't exactly sure about that. He was the town mayor, and the council did pay me a salary. I needed that money.

"No one is firing anyone," said the chief, his voice deep and rumbling with a hint of command behind it. Marcus looked so composed and manly sitting there as he leaned forward and interlaced his fingers on his desk. The memory of those large, callused, lovely strong hands holding me up last night sent heat pooling in my core.

I saw the hint of relief flicker behind his eyes, and then the smile he gave me, well, I was just about to grab the little shifter and throw him out the window to have some alone time with the chief. I let out a breath, my whole body humming as heat pounded through me.

It was all I could do not to jump over the desk and kiss the wereape. Those were some seriously hot lips. He caught me staring at them and his smile widened, which had my pulse hitting a new high.

"You burned down our gazebo," accused Gilbert, looking up at me, his brown eyes hard and full of contempt.

"I told you that was an accident."

"You did it on purpose. I saw you. You were smiling."

Had I been smiling? I couldn't remember. "I was in shock. I was aiming at the soul collector."

Gilbert pursed his lips and turned his head at Marcus. "I might not be able to fire her, but I have written to the North American Board of Merlins. Maybe they'll do it for me. She's a menace to our town. She should *not* hold a Merlin license."

"I should have let Gunner kick your owl ass."

Gilbert's face darkened for a moment, but then his eyes lit up in some sort of secret victory. "Eight thousand dollars will be deducted from your pay in equal increments over four months."

My body stiffened. "What? You can't be serious? That's an insane amount of money." I looked at the chief. "Marcus? It was an accident. Don't you have insurance for that kind of thing?" I wasn't a mathematician, but I knew that sum was close to what they paid me monthly. It would be like working for free.

Marcus dipped his head, his dark hair falling around his face and shading his eyes to make them all the more mesmerizing. The chief gave me an apologetic smile with a trace of laughter in his eyes. "Did you burn the gazebo?"

"By accident."

Marcus let out a breath, a tired look on his face.

"The town has to replace the gazebo. I'll see what I can do with the insurance. They won't pay for all of the damages, but I'm sure it'll be at least half, maybe even less, of what Gilbert is proposing."

I felt some of my tension leave. "Okay. Thanks."

Gilbert made a disgruntled, disapproving noise in his throat. "This isn't over. We'll see what the board has to say about your ruthless behavior."

I flashed him a smile. "Can't wait."

He gave me a sour look. "Disgraceful. Shameful. Train wreck."

"Incredible. Resplendent. Awesomest." That last one wasn't a word, but who cared?

The shifter looked like he'd swallowed a jar of jalapeño peppers. "Because of you, our children are going to have to miss the New Year's Eve puppet show we used to host at the gazebo. You will be called to answer for it."

I gritted my teeth to keep from telling him off and gave him a finger wave as the little shifter owl marched out of the chief's office like he was going to war.

"You shouldn't tease him. He can hold a grudge for *years*." The chief said it in a way that left me with the distinct feeling he was speaking from experience.

"If Gilbert stopped speaking to me for the rest of

my life, that would be *the* best thing to ever happen to me."

Marcus laughed as he pushed his chair back and closed the distance between us, looking great in his casual jeans and a black T-shirt.

In a rush, he wrapped an arm around my waist and pulled me against him while his other hand cupped my butt until I could feel his hard chest muscles grazing my breasts. The heat coming off of him was like a radiator. I wasn't sure if this was part of his beast or not, but I liked it. Hell, I never wanted to move.

I looked into his eyes, and my moment of passion cracked at the tension I read there. He opened his mouth but then closed it, and I could see he was struggling internally like he was trying to choose the right words.

"I'm fine," I blurted, searching his face. "I know you're worried, but I can take care of myself."

"I know."

"It's too late to go back. I'm in this. Neck-deep in it. I did this. And I have to deal with it."

"I know."

"I did what I had to do to save my gran's soul and the others."

"I know."

I cocked a brow. "I thought…" I stared at him. "That's not what you wanted to say. Is it?"

Again with that sexy as hell smile, he answered, "No." The sultry undertones in his voice yanked my thoughts back to our night of naked entanglements—and acrobatics.

My heart raced a little faster. "Then what?"

A shiver of delight went through me at his breath on my face. He licked his lips, sending a wave of heat right to my core and pulling my stomach into knots of anticipation. "What are you doing this evening?" he asked. "I know you have to be at your *other* job tonight, but I was hoping to cook you dinner at my place. And then you can tell me all about your graveyard shift."

Graveyard shift. That's pretty spot on. "You can cook?" I was impressed. I could barely make a grilled cheese without burning it. Once I tried making brownies. They came out beige.

Marcus rolled his eyes over my face. "I can."

"Is this a date? A real date? Because... I'm still not sure what this is between us."

Marcus glanced at my lips. "It is. I thought it time we had a proper date. A proper meal. A proper... dessert."

Oh, lordy, lordy. I was a lucky woman. The memory of our naked bodies intertwined flashed into my mind's eye and had heat rising from my middle to my face.

I'd never truly been inside his place. The last

time I was there, I'd stood on the threshold staring at a half-naked Allison, but I didn't want her to ruin this for me. I was excited to see his place and see how he lived. Was he a slob or was he a neat freak? I wanted to get to know him better, and this was another step closer to that—to our relationship. I wasn't sure why, but the thought made me a little nervous.

"I'll bring the wine," I told his lips. "Red or white?"

"Red."

"Okay then," I found myself saying. Nothing was sexier than a man cooking a meal for his lady.

Marcus smiled as his eyes flicked to my lips again. His head dipped and my pulse hammered in my ears while I found myself leaning in for that kiss.

But he stopped just shy, exhaling. His hot breath found the soft hollow between my ear and jaw, and my core throbbed, making me incapable of thinking about anything but his lips.

At the last moment, Marcus pulled back with that sultry smile on his face. "Good," he purred, giving my lips another look. "Be at my place by five o'clock." He let me go and stepped away, the loss of his heat hitting me like a cold shower.

I frowned. The hormones scurrying through me made my pulse thunder. He was teasing me. Fine I could do that too.

"I'll be there at five. With two wine bottles... and wearing nothing else under my coat."

The chief's jaw fell a little, heat and desire in his eyes. "It's my favorite look on you."

I laughed as heat rushed to my face. "I know."

The door to his office burst open and I flinched.

Hazmat-suit-Grace stood in the threshold. "Bleach," she said out of breath. "I need more bleach."

"I'll be right there, Grace," said the chief as he watched the older woman shuffle away. He turned back to me and said, "Five o'clock sharp. Don't be late." And with that, the chief disappeared around the corner.

In a few hours, I was going on my first official date with the chief. Well, then, I was going to make sure I looked damned hot.

I felt good, relaxed, feeling the fears and tensions of the past couple of days dissolving.

But we all know nothing this good ever lasts.

5

I stared at myself in the mirror above my new, white-washed dresser as I finished with my mascara. I did a very simple smokey eye, with a dab of lip gloss. I didn't like to wear too much makeup. With my hair down, the little black dress looked good, the hem hitting just above my knee-high boots. It was a little snug around my stomach and hips, more so than I remembered. That's what happened when you feasted on Ruth's pancakes every morning and finished the night with multiple glasses of wine.

Yeah, not giving up those.

I stood sideways and checked myself out. Whoops. A few extra inches were sprouting from my belly than before. I smiled. My mother would have noticed, and no doubt commented on my weight.

Good thing she wasn't here.

Now that my mother had left, I could go back to using her room, but somehow this new room felt more like me. House had tailored it to me, to my taste, and I found myself not wanting to switch rooms. Besides, my mother might have another fight with Sean, the man I thought was my father for nearly thirty years, so she could show up again. I had a feeling she might.

I was jittery, nervous. I didn't know why. Marcus had seen me naked with the lights on, and he thought I was beautiful. He liked the way I looked—my curves, my imperfections, all of it. Hell, the way he'd looked at me, I should be walking around naked all the time.

"You look great."

I turned to see Iris leaning against the doorframe. Dana, her album of DNA samples—from blood and toenails to strips of skin—was under her arm. Light reflected off her silky black hair, and her heart-shaped face was pulled into a smile. "He won't be able to take his eyes off of you in that dress. Good. It's how you can control him."

I let out a nervous laugh. "Why am I so nervous? I feel like a sixteen-year-old girl on her first date. It's not like I haven't been with Marcus before." I smiled at the stirring of feelings he was instilling in me.

"It's because you like him. *Really* like him. You

don't want anything to go wrong. And you don't want to be wrong about him."

I smiled at her. "You know me so well. Oh... and thanks for the gift."

Iris beamed. "You saw her?"

"I did. Was it a chicken pox curse?"

Iris arched a brow, tapping Dana. "It's my very own pimple-pox curse. You get the red, itchiness of chicken pox with a dose of pimples."

I snorted. "Well, she was pissed. It was great. Thank you."

"Anytime."

"How long will it last?" I asked.

The Dark witch shrugged. "Twenty-four hours. Maybe longer."

I glanced at the clock on my phone. "Crap. I've got to go. It's almost five." After giving myself one last look in the mirror, I rushed out of my room.

"I want details later!" called Iris as I hit the stairs.

Laughing, I reached the bottom of the stairs and hurried down the hallway to the entryway closet, the smell of coffee and spices practically making me salivate. Man, I was hungry. Catching a glimpse of Ruth at the stove made me feel a lot better. At least she wasn't sick anymore.

"You're going to sprain your ankle in those boots," called Dolores from the kitchen. "Heels are every woman's enemy. They're painful. Dangerous. And not practical at all."

"Don't listen to her, darling," argued Beverly. "Heels are a woman's best friend. There's nothing sexier and more desirable to a man than a woman in heels." She paused. "Not true. A woman in heels *and* her birthday suit is more desirable." She laughed. "Heels give you a lift. Make your butt perky. Men want perky butts and perky breasts."

"You should wear your flats," continued Dolores as I reached for my winter parka.

"In that dress?" scoffed Beverly. "She's not going to join the army in combat boots. She's going on a date. Please. It's not only a fashion faux pas but a sex faux pas. Heels get you laid."

I rolled my eyes. Oh, boy. Here we go.

"That is not true," disputed Dolores. "To hear you talk like that, you're assuming women wear heels because otherwise, they won't get sex? Ridiculous."

"Do you wear heels?" prompted Beverly.

"I prefer flats."

"And when was the last time you got laid?"

Silence.

I couldn't see it, but I could almost feel the scowl on Dolores's face.

"Exactly my point," stated Beverly happily at Dolores's reticence, and I recognized Ruth's snort.

The ladies are back, I thought, smiling.

"But she has to work later tonight," said Dolores, and I heard the discomfort in her voice. "She can't do *that* job looking like *that*."

"I'll be back to change. Don't worry," I called back, realizing I'd forgotten to mention the suit Jack had me wear. Dolores was right about one thing. No way in hell was I going to wear heels tonight.

I was glad they were out of their bedrooms and doing what they did best—arguing. Part of me wanted to stay. I enjoyed my aunts' company immensely. But the thought of being alone with Marcus was too good to pass up.

I looped my bag over my head, grabbed my leather gloves, and called out, "I'll see you later."

The rest of their arguments were lost as I shut the door behind me and started down the sidewalk. After the fifth step, I slipped but caught myself before I fell. Okay, maybe heels in the snow wasn't one of my best ideas, but it was too late to turn back now. Next time, screw the sexiness. I'd go with practicality.

With baby steps, I managed to continue down the sidewalk without falling on my face, which was an acrobatic performance in itself. I even threw in a few ballerina pirouettes and a few penchés as I maneuvered my way carefully. At this rate, I would never make it to Marcus's place on time. If I went any faster, I'd slip and probably sprain both ankles. Why didn't I take the Volvo?

There was only one thing left for me to do.

Time to ride the ley lines.

I realized this might mean a visit from my dear ol' dad. I wanted to know so much, to ask a million questions, but I didn't have time. Not now. It wasn't the evening to start our daughter-father bonding. It would have to wait.

I'd wanted to avoid using the ley lines for a little while, but this was an emergency. Not really, but you get the point.

Pushing out my will, I reached out to the nearest ley line and pulled it to me, willing it forward until it was right there with me. A sudden blast of power shuddered around me, unleashing a flow of energy that thrummed in the air.

I stilled myself, holding it there, readying to jump—

"Tessa."

I flinched at the familiarity of the voice. It belonged to someone who had supposedly left.

The ley line's power left me in a rush. I blinked, turned, and said, "Mom?"

Amelia Davenport stood on the sidewalk behind me. Her gray wool coat and a matching scarf wrapped around her, fitting her perfectly. Panting, with her cheeks pink, she looked like she'd run to catch up with me.

"I thought you left?" I didn't care to hide the surprise in my voice, nor the harshness. The witch had left without a word. I thought it hadn't affected me that much, but apparently, it did.

My mother looked over her shoulder like she thought she'd been followed. Weird, even for her. Her dark eyes met mine again. "I did, but I came back. I came back because I needed to talk to you." Her eyes flicked to my legs. "You'll kill yourself walking in those in the middle of winter. You should have worn flat boots and taken your heels in a bag to wear later."

"Thanks for the tip, Mom. I thought you'd be with da—Sean by this time. What did you want to tell me? Better make it quick. I'm late for my date." It was a strange thing to unlearn something you thought was the truth for nearly thirty years. It would take some getting used to. Sean was not my father. Obi-Wan Kenobi was.

Again my mother glanced over her shoulder. "I want to talk to you about Obiryn."

My brows shot to my hairline. "Obi who?"

My mother exhaled loudly. "Obiryn. Your father."

"Ah. Obi-Wan Kenobi. I get it now. Obi... Obiryn..." So, that was his real name. Obiryn.

"Is he still using that name?" My mother laughed. "Well. It doesn't matter."

"So, you're fully admitting that my father is a demon?"

My mother waved her gloved hands at me. "Yes. Yes. You need to listen to me."

I crossed my arms over my chest, not appreciating her giving me orders. "When did you two hook up? Before or after Sean?" I needed some answers. And since Obi had flatly refused to give them, I was going to make mother dearest instead.

"Before," answered my mother, shaking her head. "I met Obiryn two years before your father."

"Was it just sex? I'm not judging. Just want to know the truth."

My mother glared at me. "I'm not Beverly. I don't throw myself at every handsome eligible man."

"Demon."

"What?"

"You said, man. But daddy's a demon. You know... red skin and talons and horns."

My mother let out a puff of air. "Why do you always have to do this?"

I shrugged. "I find it strange that you, magic hater, would hook up with a demon. It's a lot to process."

My mother had the nerve to look offended. "I'm not a magic hater."

"Magic disliker. Magic abstainer. Call it what you want, but we all know how you feel about it. You even tried to make me hate it too, but it didn't work. You couldn't scare the magic out of me."

My mother stared at me for a moment. "You're so much like him, you know. Even as a baby, I could see him in you."

I squinted my eyes. "Not sure if that's a compliment or an insult." I pursed my lips. "Probably an insult, coming from you."

"I did love Obiryn," said my mother as though I hadn't spoken. "I didn't know what he was at first. He didn't tell me. He led me to believe he was a witch. Eventually, he did tell me. I was so confused. I was young. I left him, and then that's when I met Sean." She exhaled loudly. "You know the rest. I was pregnant when I married Sean."

"Nice. Did he know?" I bet he did. It would explain why I was always left behind.

"Yes. Sean is a great man. I know you don't think so, but he is. He took you in even though you weren't his. Raised you like you were his own child."

"He didn't raise me. He didn't do anything." My temper flared. I didn't want to hear about my mother's paramours. "I don't really care who you're with. If Sean makes you happy, that's great. Be with Sean. Be happy. I need to go."

"I'm not finished," my mother yelled. I'd turned to leave, but the fear in her voice made me stop.

Panic flicked across her features, the same panic I'd seen when I'd told her I'd used the ley lines. "What's going on? Does this have something to do with the ley lines?"

Her shoulders stiffened at the mention of the ley lines. "Don't you understand? Why all those years I kept you from doing magic? I thought if I could turn you against it... it would keep you safe. It would all go away."

My anger growing, I squared my shoulders. "What are you saying? That you protected me all those years? From magic? I seriously doubt that." Not to mention all the times she'd forgotten to pick me up from school or forgot to buy groceries for the week so I was left to eat Corn Flakes for breakfast, lunch, and dinner for five days. She wasn't protecting me from anything. She'd just forgotten about me. Now, well, she just sounded crazy.

"I kept you from doing magic to protect you," she said, her voice a mix of anger and fear.

I stared at my mother, looking for signs that she was under the influence, but her eyes were bright and focused. "You think Obiryn wants to harm me? You're not making any sense." My demon father had sacrificed a part of his soul for me. I would never forget that. If he'd wanted me dead, he would have left me with the soul collector.

"No." My mother shook her head. "Not Obiryn. The others."

"The others. What others?" Yup. She was losing her mind.

I heard a sudden loud honk and turned to see a man's irritated face behind the wheel of a gray SUV. Through the window, I could see he was still sporting that ugly beard and man-bun that was out of style now, which looked ridiculous on him. Well, that was a surprise. I glared back at him. Now that I knew he wasn't my father, I could afford to throw him a few glares and scowls, maybe even a few curses.

The next thing that happened was an even bigger surprise.

My mother grabbed me by the shoulders and pulled me into a hug. I was so shocked that I just stood there with my arms hanging awkwardly at my sides while my mother did all the hugging. Well, hugging is a bit much, it was more of a two-second clumsy upper body bump.

She stepped back and said, "Be safe. And I'm sorry."

I stared at her. "Who are you?"

My mother didn't wave goodbye as she jumped into the front passenger seat next to Sean. I stared as the SUV disappeared down the street, gawking at the woman, witch, who I apparently hardly knew. That had been our first hug. I couldn't remember ever being hugged by her before.

I'd always thought I knew my mother well. I could always read her and knew what to expect. Clearly, I'd been wrong.

Amelia Davenport was a mystery to me.

6

"I know I'm late. I'm so sorry," I prattled on. "But you see, I ran into my mother. And she told me some pretty incredible stuff. I don't even believe half of what she told me." My eyes widened suddenly. "Crap. I forgot the wine. Give me a second and I'll go get some."

Marcus reached out and grabbed my hand, which was like an instant shutoff of my brain. All my focus went to the heat radiating from his hand at his touch. "Slow down," laughed the chief, his smile infectious and startling. I'd forgotten for a moment how incredibly handsome he was. "I've got lots of wine. Come in. Let me get you a glass. Red, right?"

"Yes."

"Here, give me your coat." Marcus stepped behind me, his breath hot against my neck, and my skin erupted into goose bumps. His hands brushed the back of my neck as he gently tugged my parka, and something was incredibly intimate about him standing so close behind me. Either that or my hormones were out of whack again.

Marcus hung my coat in the closet off to the side. "Come and sit. I'll get you that wine."

Once I'd pulled off my sexy and unpractical knee-high boots, I followed him into the kitchen barefoot. Barefoot! Shit. I glanced down at my feet and winced at the state of my toes. It was like someone had taken a cheese grater to them, the remnants of old nail polish half on, half off. Good god. I had sasquatch feet.

Seriously, though. When did I have time to pamper myself? Never. I pulled my toes in as far as I could, hoping Marcus was too busy with cooking to notice my pedicure disaster.

"Why are you walking like that?"

Apparently, I was wrong. "Cold feet. Stupid boots. I like your place," I said, switching the conversation away from my toes. Men don't care about toes. Right?

"Thanks." Marcus pulled out a bottle of wine from behind his kitchen island.

I took the opportunity to look around, my nose filling with the smells of cooking and spices. It was an open concept with kitchen, dining, and living areas all in one large space, yet each was defined in their designated spots. A dark brown leather couch and two thick chairs sat atop a tribal rug. The dining room table and chairs were all made of dark chunky wood with more of a mountain cabin vibe. It was very male but tastefully decorated and comfortable. It reminded me of those cabins I'd seen in the Allegheny Tionesta Creek Camping site. I hadn't noticed the furniture the last time I was here. Allison had made sure of that. All I remembered seeing were her long bare legs and Marcus's bare chest.

Two rooms sat off the living area and I spotted a large bathroom. His place was clean and fresh. The lighting was low, comfortable, and sexy. Obviously, this wasn't the first time he'd had a woman over, and I wasn't talking about Allison.

"Here."

I turned around and took the large glass of wine from Marcus's hand. "If I drink all that, I'll be too drunk to get any souls tonight." I laughed. "Maybe that's a good thing."

Marcus lost some of his smile. "Come sit at the kitchen island. Dinner'll be ready in a few minutes. You can tell me all about your new job while I finish up." His tension rose, the muscles on his neck flexing. He was worried about me. Was it wrong that it turned me on? Hell no.

I followed him—his butt really—to the kitchen

and sat on one of the stools. An assortment of olives, cheeses, and loaves of bread was spread along the light gray stone counter, all within reach.

My heart raced. I was nervous and felt like every nerve ending in my body pulsed into a burn. I wasn't exactly sure why I was nervous, though. Maybe it was because I felt this relationship had all the signs pointing to something serious, and it terrified me. The old me would have probably made an excuse and run away. But the new me wasn't afraid of commitment, even if it meant I might get hurt. I wanted to explore this and see where our relationship would go.

Letting go of some of my tension, I popped a kalamata olive into my mouth. "I love olives and cheese," I said between chews. With his back to me, I stared at his tight butt in those jeans, remembering how good it looked without them. His hands moved around the pots on the stove, making the muscles on his back pop and slide beneath his white T-shirt. I could sit here all night and watch that show.

"I know," said the chief with his head turned slightly to the side so I could see his smile.

I frowned skeptically at him. "You've been investigating me, chief? That's a little pervy."

Marcus laughed. "Maybe."

I took a small sip of wine, letting my taste buds tango with my tongue. It was marvelous. I had to be careful not to drink too much. Just the thought of what I was supposed to be doing later had my stomach churning.

I placed my glass on the counter. "Smells amazing. What are you making?"

Marcus turned around and said, "Vegetable Tikka Masala, sweet potato curry, and veggie biryani. I know you don't like meat. You like Indian food, though. Right? Or did my spies get that wrong?"

Wow. "You had me at sweet potato curry."

The chief laughed, and it made the butterflies in my stomach high-five. I could get used to that laugh. Hell, I wanted to make it into a cream and rub it all over my body.

Marcus turned his gray eyes on me. The look of desire in him sent adrenaline to my core, rousing me. "I love to cook. Among other things." The way he'd said the last part had heat pounding in my middle. I knew what he was talking about. He did those "other things" to me a few nights ago—over and over again. Just the thought of those other things nearly had me flying over the kitchen island and tackling that handsome bastard.

I swallowed, trying to stifle my lady hormones. "Good to know." I took a big gulp of my wine before I could stop myself. "Stop staring at me like that."

Marcus blinked, but it did nothing to wipe away the lust I saw there. "I can't help it. You're beautiful."

I snorted in my wine. Splashes of red liquid hit my nose and cheeks. Yeah. Not very beautiful. But thankfully Marcus had turned away and didn't see my humiliation.

While I sat there watching this virile man cook me dinner, I realized my ex had never once, in the five years we were together, cooked me dinner or anything really. And it felt amazing to be treated this way, like I was special, like a queen. A witch could get used to that.

"You can go sit at the table. It's ready," ordered the chief.

Doing as I was instructed, I grabbed my wine and picked one of the two spots that were already fitted with plates and cutlery.

Once seated, Marcus came over and set three large bowls of steaming goodness in the middle of the table with extra-large serving spoons.

"I'm impressed," I told him as he set the opened bottle of red wine with the label of Rufino Chianti on the table with an empty glass. I watched as he then took my plate and began filling it up with a bit of everything. "Are you being this extra nice because you want your *dessert*?" I teased. Who was I kidding? I wanted dessert too. Double banana split with rocky road ice cream.

"Maybe." He handed me my plate, filled his, and sat in the chair facing me. "I hope you like it."

"If it tastes as good as it smells, I will." I laughed. "I have a feeling I won't be able to get out of this dress. I should have put on my Thanksgiving pants."

"Thanksgiving pants?"

"You know... the ones with the elastic waist. So I can actually *eat* the food and not just stare at it..." I stopped myself before furthering my humiliation. Marcus's forehead had creased in the middle as he listened to me. What the hell was wrong with me? You don't tell the guy you're hot for about your "fat pants." If I could bend my leg high enough and kick myself in the ass, I would.

Marcus threw back his head and laughed.

"Great. You think I'm hilarious." I loved the sound of his laugh. I really did. Just not when his laughter was directed at me.

"I do." He poured some more wine in my glass expertly, not a single drop dribbling from the top. "Don't worry," he said, his gray eyes pinning me again. "I can get you out of that dress."

Heat rushed to my face. The way he'd said it was like he'd done it a million times before. And surprisingly, it didn't bother me.

"You did promise to only wear your winter coat," he said.

I did. I blinked. "You want me to strip now? Can I try the potatoes first?"

Marcus filled his wine glass and then held it over to me. "To you," he said, his voice low and sultry. "I'm so happy to have met you. You make me crazy sometimes, but it's a good crazy. I haven't felt this alive in a very long time."

I smiled and tapped his glass with mine. "Careful what you wish for."

We spent the rest of the evening laughing and talking, enjoying each other's company. I was comfortable with him, something I had never felt before with a man. I felt I could be myself with him —the real me. I could tell him anything and he wouldn't judge me. I made sure not to talk about the soul collection thing, not until I had my dessert. What? Trust me. You wouldn't want to ruin the mood either.

And, boy oh boy, could the wereape cook.

At first, I tried not to moan whenever my fork reached my mouth. But after the second mouthful, I let it all out.

"Oh, my god, this is so good," I moaned, enjoying the blasts of curry spices in my mouth. "I'm surprised there isn't a line of starving, available women outside your door."

Marcus took a sip of his wine. "I don't cook for

everyone. Only on special occasions. And only for someone special."

Delicious tingles washed over my body at his meaning. I might not have the ability to detect lies, but I was experienced enough to know he wasn't delivering a line. He meant it. Every word.

"You've got something on your mouth... right there..." Marcus reached over and, with his napkin, wiped the corner of my mouth, gently tugging. All the while he stared at my lips, his mouth slightly open like he was contemplating whether or not to crush his lips on mine. My heart pounded, sending waves of demand pulsing through me. I froze where I was, afraid if I moved, he would go away. He was breathless with his passion held in check.

Our eyes locked. His eyes sparkled with desire and need.

Dessert, here I come!

"You finished?" he asked as he rose from his seat, his eyes never leaving mine.

I pushed my chair back and stood. "If you mean you're about to rip off my dress to expose my nakedness, then yeah, I'm finished."

Expression heavy with the knowledge of what was to come, he leaned closer and scooped me up into his arms, his mouth crushing against mine while letting a low guttural sound escape him. His tongue found mine and heat spilled like molten lava through me to my groin.

"Couch!" I squealed in delight, pulling my mouth away for only a fraction of a second. Forget the bedroom. I was about to explode like a hormonal piñata.

"Yes, ma'am." Laughing, Marcus swung me around in the direction of the living room.

He lowered me on the couch, the leather smooth under my hands and back. Next, his eyes blazing with lust, he grabbed the front of my dress with his manly hands, and with the sound of fabric tearing— ripped it off.

I stared at my exposed bra and panties. "Damn. You weren't kidding about getting me out of this dress," I laughed.

"Ooops," he said, his smile sly and not looking a bit bothered. "I thought it was a wrap dress."

"Faux wrap dress," I said, surprised that he actually knew what a wrap dress was.

"I'll buy you another one." Smiling seductively, he tugged his t-shirt over his head, exposing those wonderful, perfect, rippling muscles under that golden skin.

"Sure. Whatever," I answered, not caring about the dress or anything else but getting my freak on with the chief before I combusted into flames.

His weight was a welcomed warmth pressing on

me as he leaned over me and pushed me down until my head was on the back of the couch.

I reached for his belt buckle, fumbling with it until I pulled it free and went to work on the zipper of his jeans. I yanked hard. I might have ruined the zipper. Who cared?

I felt Marcus's rough, callused hands work down to my hips, hook the edges of my underwear, and pull—

The door to his apartment burst open.

"Oh. Am I interrupting something?" Allison stood in the entryway, where she had a clear, unobstructed view of my panties and everything else.

Under a thick layer of foundation, I could still see a multitude of red spots over her face. Even so, her expression looked like she'd just won the Lottery. Swell.

"What the hell, Allison?" growled Marcus. "You can't just show up unannounced. You don't live here anymore." He glared at her, not at all concerned about the large, hard bulge that tented the front of his jeans.

When I saw her smile widen at the sight of my half-naked body, heat flamed to my face and I tugged my torn dress around me. But her eyes said it all. She was thrilled to have interrupted what was about to happen.

"It's Grace," said the tall blonde. "She's collapsed."

Deep fear pinched his eyes. "Where is she?"

"At the office," said Allison as her eyes met mine. "It doesn't look good."

A phone call was all it took, but Allison had decided to show up in person. I knew she'd done this on purpose. Somehow, she'd found out about our date.

She sounded really sincere. Even her face showed the right amount of emotions. But then I saw it. Just when Marcus reached down to grab his T-shirt—that split-second hint of a shark smile on her face when she looked at me like she'd gotten what she came for.

She'd orchestrated this. I wouldn't put it past her to make Grace sick on purpose to ruin our date.

When Allison then looked at Marcus in a way that suggested previous carnal knowledge, I wanted to fry her on the spot.

Marcus pulled on his T-shirt and zipped up his jeans. "Tessa. I'm sorry. But I have to go check on Grace."

"Of course, you do," I told him, hiding the disappointment from my voice.

He leaned over me and gave me a quick kiss. "I'll make it up to you. Promise."

"It's fine. I have to get ready for tonight anyway." I

found myself nodding as he pulled away and I stood up, careful to keep my dress wrapped around me, my face hot with anger.

Marcus watched me for a long moment. "Be safe."

I let out a breath. "I will. Call me when you know more about Grace."

Marcus gave a nod as he moved to the entry closet and grabbed his coat. After he pulled on his boots, he disappeared out the door, the sound of his heavy body echoing down the steps.

I looked away and found Allison watching me with that same winning smile on her smug face. She stared at me for a beat longer and then fled after the chief.

I let out a puff of angry air as the door slammed shut. Okay, I had to give it to her. That was pretty creative. Allison might have won this fight in her attempt to take Marcus from me.

But this wasn't over.

"Bring it on, gorilla Barbie."

7

I stood on the sidewalk next to Davenport House under a dark, cloudy sky, the cold air lifting the hair off of my shoulders. Only this time I wasn't wearing my sexy little black dress. I was wearing my mothball-smelling soul-collecting outfit. Yippee.

I wrinkled my nose. Letting it air out in my room all day had done nothing to suppress the smell of mothballs with a hint of sulfur. I wondered if the smell had something to do with the way it let me travel from different worlds. Maybe it did. Maybe it had to stink to work.

My mind was restless. It kept going from what my mother had said to tonight's job of soul collecting—Janet Purcell's soul, to be exact. The thought brought bile rising in the back of my throat.

And then there was Allison.

She might have succeeded in ruining my "sexy time" with Marcus, but she had nothing on the spectacular date we'd shared. The conversations, the laughter, the connection had been the best date I'd ever been on. So she could suck it.

It had been ten o'clock sharp just moments ago when I left my cell phone on the side table in the entryway before stepping out. Jack hadn't given me a specific time to meet him again, nor did he give me a designated spot either. I figured I'd just stand where he'd showed up last night.

"You better show up soon, Jack," I told the empty space in front of me. "I'm not freezing my ass out here for you or anyone."

And just when I pulled my hair back into a low ponytail, I felt a pop of displaced air.

About four feet from me stood a tall man in a dark suit and hat who hadn't been there a moment ago. Hairless and thin, it looked like his pale skin had been painted over bone.

The soul collector pulled out his pocket watch. "Excellent. I appreciate the promptness." He dropped his watch inside his jacket. "You look flushed. Have you been running?"

I scowled at him. "It's cold."

Jack threw his gaze around. "Ah, yes. It's winter here. You're not exactly dressed for it."

"I'm wearing your damn suit."

His jaw opened in sudden understanding. "Are you ready?"

"No." I felt ill.

"Better get a move on, Tessa Davenport." Jack gestured with his briefcase to a spot next to him on the sidewalk. "You know the drill," he added with a laugh.

Kill me now. My time to suck it up. I stepped next to the soul collector, and then my world faded to black.

Okay. The second time world-jumping with the demon was still out-of-this-world mind-blowing but not as frightening as the first time. I knew what to expect now, so at least I was prepared.

The pulling of my body in every direction at once was expected, but it still scared the crap out of me. I could handle the darkness as I drifted along. I even tried to spy on Jack to see if he was flying in a superhero pose next to me, but only endless blackness was all around.

The pulling stopped just as abruptly as it started. The darkness lifted and my feet hit solid ground. Swallowing the intense feeling of vertigo, I looked around.

I saw white walls, smelled the overwhelming scent of disinfectant and ammonia, and heard the constant, whisper of beeps from machines. Lots of tiles and fluorescent lights flickered feebly while long shadows stretched out from doors and hallways.

We weren't in someone's house. We were in a hospital. Scratch that. We were in a hospital room.

I turned on the spot. A woman lay in a single bed with thin white sheets covering her small frame. Her scalp showed through a few strings of long white hair. She looked like a mummified corpse whose skin was paper-thin, cracked, and flaky. A tube rested just below her nose with two small prongs going inside her nostrils. Her eyes were closed, and for a second I thought she was dead, but then her chest rose and fell.

"Here you are." Jack handed me a scroll of paper that looked similar to the one I'd seen him show Xander.

I took it. "What's this?" I asked, unfurling the parchment, though I already knew. My eyes skimmed through the wording. "It's a contract. Janet Purcell's." I saw her name printed clearly at the bottom next to her signature.

"Indeed it is." Jack smiled at me, his teeth a startling white against the dim light of the room.

I looked up at the woman, Janet Purcell, to see if she'd heard us, but her eyes were still closed. Maybe I'd get lucky and she was in a coma? Wishful thinking. There were no flowers, no cards, no sign that this woman had any family.

My stomach lurched when I read the contract again. "She gave you her soul in exchange for the unconditional love from someone called Albert Harper. It's dated nearly sixty years ago."

Crap. This poor woman gave her soul to a demon to have the man she loved love her back. I didn't think I'd be capable of something like that, but I could see how easily women and men would agree to that kind of contract. Horror trickled through me. This was so wrong.

Jack raised his chin proudly. "Right you are, Tessa Davenport. You can read. How wonderful."

"Tessa."

"I'm sorry?"

"Just call me Tessa."

"Well then, Tessa." The demon smiled delightedly at me, making my stomach twist. "It's your turn to collect the soul." To my utter horror, Jack handed me his briefcase.

"Like hell I am." I shook my head and took a step back. "No way. I'm not touching that." To me, touching that briefcase would seal the deal. It would make me like Jack. It would make me a soul collector.

I stood my ground, crossing my arms over my chest as though somehow that made it final. "No. You can hold your own damn briefcase."

Lines formed on the demon's brow. "You will. You must. All soul collectors and those in their employ use a briefcase. Unless you want your grandmother's soul and all the others you traded your services for to be back in my charge? No? Well then. You're in my servitude. Take it." He shoved his briefcase at me.

Wincing, I grabbed it with my free hand, holding it away from my body like it had a bomb inside and was about to detonate.

I wasn't sure what to expect. Maybe a burn to the touch? But then I did feel something. My breath caught as I felt a cold hum of energy like an electrical current running through my fingertips to my toes and the top of my head.

Power. Demonic power.

"Well," said a woman as she walked in wearing a blue nurse's uniform. "You finally decided to show up." She frowned at me.

"Excuse me?" I said, a bit taken aback by her tone. I let the briefcase hang next to my hip.

"She's been in here for four months," said the nurse. "Not one of you ever came to see her. Not even after her husband Mr. Harper died last week." She eyed us suspiciously. "Visiting hours are over, but I'll make an exception."

Shit. She thought we're her ungrateful family. I felt even worse now that my suspicions had been revealed. This poor woman was alone—sick and probably dying and alone.

I glowered at Jack, telling him with my eyes that I was going to get him back for this. But he pretended not to notice and kept staring at the nurse as though he liked her outfit. Either that, or he was thinking up ways to con her for her soul.

"Janet?" The nurse pressed a gentle hand on the old woman. "Janet, wake up. You have visitors." The nurse waited until Janet's eyes flickered open, and then she stepped back, glared at me and Jack, and then gave us the room.

When my gaze found Janet again, her eyes were wide open and filled with fear. Awesome. I knew this was going to be awesome.

"I hate this job," I mumbled.

"I love this job," said Jack brightly. "Go on then. You must present the contract and the soul..." Jack checked his pocket watch, "will be yours in twenty-five seconds."

Janet whimpered and when I looked over to her, she was shaking her head.

My eyes warmed as my emotions ran from one extreme to the other. My thoughts went to Gran and the others. It was the only thing that kept me from running the hell out of this hospital. *I had to do this.*

I kept telling myself the woman had known what

she'd signed. She had offered her soul willingly in exchange for love.

Only it didn't make me feel any better.

I glared at Jack again. "How is it the nurse can see you? I get that Janet can since she summoned you years ago. But the nurse?" I knew that most humans did not have the sight to see the paranormal around them. It begged the question how this nurse could see him.

Jack grinned, clearly in a good mood. "Because I chose to make myself visible to the Unseeing. One of the perks of being a soul collector."

"As what?" I asked, guessing that Jack had many faces. He probably went with one that was the most trustworthy, like a jolly old man who looked like Santa or something.

His hairless brow rose. "Why, me, of course. Who else?"

Right.

With the contract in one hand and the briefcase in the other, I looked over my shoulder to the hallway beyond the door to see if anyone was looking. But it was deserted. Swallowing down my nerves, I moved to stand next to Janet and placed the briefcase on the bed.

"You must open the briefcase," instructed Jack, annoying me further.

Gritting my teeth, I opened the briefcase and

looked at Janet, her round eyes on my face. I cleared my throat and held the contract in my trembling fingers. "I'm sorry about this," I whispered. "If there was a way I could somehow make this go away, I would."

"That's not what it says in the contract," hissed Jack, standing behind me and making me flinch. "Ten seconds."

Tears fell from the corners of Janet's eyes, and it took everything I had not to start bawling along with her. I hated my life. I hated myself at this moment.

I felt warmth on my hand, and when I looked at the bed, I found Janet's hand on mine. She didn't say a word. She only patted my hand in a way that said it was okay, her face drawn and filled with sorrow. Her eyes weren't round with fear but filled with understanding. She was permitting me to take her soul.

My lips trembled. "I'm going to hell."

"We don't call it hell. We call it the Netherworld," instructed Jack.

I wasn't sure if I should read the contract or not. I didn't think I could, not with my eyes brimming with tears and my body shaking like a leaf in a hurricane.

"The contract is for backup," stated the demon, having sensed my hesitation. "Proof of signage in case you find yourself in a debate with one of our clients. You don't need to read it."

I didn't even realize I had taken Janet's hand in

mine until I felt her go still. I looked up and squinted at the sudden burst of light, just as Janet's body glittered, covered in brilliant white light. I blinked at the hovering ball of light—her soul—and then the gleaming globe shot past me and disappeared inside the briefcase. With a clap, the briefcase snapped shut on its own.

"Well done, Tessa," praised the demon. "You're a natural. Not that I doubted your abilities. I knew you would be. Then again… I am an excellent teacher."

When I looked back at Janet, her eyes were closed, and her expression was frozen in a mix between fear and regret. I didn't have to check her pulse to know she'd passed. My stomach rolled. One thing was for sure. I didn't want to be here when the nurse came back. Because… that would be bad.

"Well, then." Jack pulled his shoulders back. "Now that I know you can handle yourself, we can continue. The rest will be a breeze."

I spun around, bent over a small metal garbage bin next to the bed, and hurled. Once I stopped gagging, I straightened and wiped my mouth.

"You call this handling myself? This is the *worst* thing I've ever done. It's not a breeze. It's torture."

"Nonsense." Jack dismissed me with a wave of his skeletal hand. "She was old. Dying. The woman had no more teeth. You did her a favor. Just think about it. Now her soul has purpose."

I glared at the demon. "After my contract is over, I'm going to kill you."

Jack laughed like it was the funniest thing he'd ever heard as he adjusted his hat over his bald head. "Don't forget your briefcase." He gestured to the bed. He raised his chin and sniffed. "The night is young and full of souls. Hurry up now. There's work to be done."

I grabbed the briefcase from Janet's side, wanting to smash it against Jack's head. I looked at her face one last time and nearly threw up again. When I turned back to the soul collector, he had another, exact briefcase in his hand.

I shook my head. "Figures."

"What was that?" asked the demon.

"I hate you."

"Of course you do," answered the demon in a matter-of-fact tone. "I wouldn't expect it any other way. No one likes their boss. It's a universal rule."

I pursed my lips. "Sounds like you're speaking from experience."

Jack said nothing as he left the room. I followed him out and stepped into the hallway of the hospital, thinking there was more to this demon than I knew.

Clean white halls and white walls met me as I looked around at the fluorescent lights flickering from above.

A nurse's station sat across from us, and the

sound of fingers typing on a keyboard reached me as I watched the same nurse behind the station typing away. We were right across from her, but she didn't glance up.

I was suddenly hit with a wave of fatigue, and I hadn't even done anything. Well, not really. Not if you counted removing Janet's soul from her body and stuffing it in my briefcase—*my* briefcase. I would never get used to that.

The demon raised his chin again and sniffed like he was a blood hound on a scent. "We need to go up two floors," he told me. "The fourth floor smells of desperation and death. That's where we need to be." He made a sound of pleasure in his throat. "I'll never tire of that smell. The smell of despair and helplessness."

I frowned. "You're one nasty piece of work."

Jack inclined his head. "Hospitals are a soul collector's gold mine. Hundreds of sick, dilapidated mortals clinging to life by a thread." He smiled like this was a good thing. "Sick mortals are desperate mortals, and they'll agree to anything."

I felt my jaw fall somewhere on the tile floor around my feet. "You've got to be joking."

Jack tugged on the sleeves of his jacket. "Demons don't joke. We make deals."

I knew it. I was going to be sick again. Preferably all over Jack. "You're going to go around this hospital and prey on the sick for their souls? I can't even begin to wrap my head around how wrong this is. It's foul and really messed up."

"Who said anything about me?" Jack smiled, a slip of teeth showing. "I'm not the one. You are."

My face went cold.

Yeah, definitely going to hell.

8

The fourth floor was graveyard silent without a flicker of sound from the staff or even the muffled noise from a television. I hadn't spotted a single nurse or doctor as Jack and I stalked the hallways. A sign on the wall, in bold black letters, read: PALLIATIVE CARE.

Three hours later, I had twenty-three new contracts. I wasn't sure if it was because I was a woman or that my face wasn't as scary as the soul collector's, but somehow the humans I came in contact with kept on agreeing to the terms of the contracts, and the souls just kept on coming.

The sick, the desperate—men and women, it didn't matter—as soon as I told them who I was (a soul collector in training, according to Jack) and that I could take away their illness (again according to

Jack) they all agreed to sign. Well, not all of them. Some of them screamed. Some of them laughed and told me to take my crap elsewhere. But I was surprised at the number who were very willing to sign.

At first, I was a little bit freaked. These were humans, and most humans thought the paranormal world was just make-believe. The closest thing to the supernatural to hit them were the *Twilight* movies.

All the while Jack hung back, hovering like a teacher who was making sure his student didn't mess up.

"Do you agree to the terms?" I asked the fifty-year-old man, lying in his bed, whose name was Bob. His cancer had done a real number on him, and he looked like a frail ninety-year-old about to take his last breath.

Bob blinked up at me. "And I'll be cancer-free?" he wheezed, as though just speaking took a tremendous effort. "For the rest of my life?"

"Yes. But your soul will belong to the soul collector once you've reached the end of your long life. Do you understand?"

Bob's eyes were wet with a thin film over them. "Okay. Yes. I'll sign."

I shifted uneasily. These humans had no idea what they were signing, not really. And Jack's contract made sure of that.

"I don't think you fully understand what that means," I said as the images of Gran's soul being tortured by some giant horned demon flashed in my mind's eye. "Your soul will belong to a *demon*. Demons eat—"

"Thank you, Tessa." Jack grabbed my arm and thrust me behind him, none too gently, but I wasn't giving up that easily.

I pushed my way forward, hitting Jack with my hip until I was next to Bob's bed again. "They'll torture your soul. They will do whatever they want to it." Yes, I was aware Jack would probably torture me after this, but I couldn't let this go. I couldn't leave out any information. They needed to make an informed decision.

Jack sighed loudly through his nose, his face screwed up in a false smile. "He said he's going to sign it. You can stop now. Though your pitch needs refining," said the demon, giving me his version of "angry eyes."

From inside his jacket, Jack yanked out a new contract and handed it to the man who was dying of cancer. "Sign at the bottom, Bob, and you will be right as rain. Cancer-free," he added as a pen magically appeared in his long, thin fingers.

While Bob signed his contract, I turned to Jack. "Do the contracts just magically appear in your jacket pockets? How does that work?"

Jack grinned. "One step at a time, Tessa."

A thought occurred to me. "Soul collectors can't just cross over to the mortal world to con the dying out of their souls. No one conjured you. How is it possible that you can do this," I asked, waving my hands around.

"You're forgetting that I *was* summoned. Janet Purcell summoned me sixty years ago. And by doing so, and signing her contract, I am able to... as you say... cross over."

"Yeah, but these people never summoned you."

"No, they did not. But once I've crossed, I can stay for as long as I like."

"Until the sun rises."

Jack nodded his head. "Until the sun rises."

"I signed it. When do I start feeling better?" asked Bob, the pen slipping from his weak fingers.

"We must shake on it," said Jack, smiling at Bob like this was nothing, but I knew better.

Jack reached out and shook the man's hand. I saw a spark of light, the same light I'd seen when my father and Jack had shaken hands back in the in-between. The spark imprinted on Bob's soul and promised it to the soul collector.

"Thank you for your business," said Jack as he snatched up the contract and slipped it inside his jacket.

I took a step back and waited.

And then just like the other twenty-three humans, Bob's face went through a whirlwind of expressions: fear, disbelief, acceptance, and finally hope.

His face and his body transformed in front of me —literally.

His cheeks plumped up first, giving him a younger appearance. Next his eyes, which were brown, cleared. The hair part always freaked me out. Like, fast-forward footage of a plant growing from the National Geographic channel, brown and gray hair sprouted from the top of Bob's bald head until it was full of hair.

Smiling, Bob yanked off his bed sheets and jumped to the ground. He even started to jog on the spot, not kidding.

"This is unbelievable! It's a miracle!" he yelled and then ran out the room, his white butt showing through the gap of his thin hospital gown.

"It's not," I whispered. "Not even close." It was demon magic. And now his soul belonged to one.

Feeling like a fraud, I turned to Jack. "I'd like to go home now. I'm done for tonight." Obviously, Jack was the decision-maker, but I didn't think I could do one more soul robbing, which was exactly how it felt.

Jack smiled proudly. "You've done well tonight,

Tessa. I believe this will do. There's just one more thing to do, and then you can retire for the night."

I didn't like the jovial innuendo in his voice. "What's that?"

Jack pulled his fedora tightly over his head and then glanced at me. "We must bring Janet's soul to my locker."

"We?" Oh shit. Not this again.

Before I could refuse, the soul collector stepped next to me, and the darkness took me.

It really did this time. It took me like a heavy black blanket swathing me until that's all there was. Blackness. And then *more* blackness.

If we were off to Jack's locker, I knew what was coming. Pain. Lots and lots of pain.

It had hurt like hell the last time I'd been in the in-between, or Jack's locker, as he liked to call it. It wasn't a realm for the living. Yet, I was alive this time.

Again, there was no pain while traveling, just a constant feeling of being pulled like every cell in my body had detached itself, only to come together at the very last moment. I assumed it was just another perk from my mothball-smelling suit. It seemed to be the glue that kept my body together.

My feet hit solid ground. I didn't collapse, but I did feel like my world was spinning as a wave of nausea hit like I'd just stepped off the fastest merry-go-round in the history of merry-go-rounds.

Once the dizziness subsided, I glanced around. It looked exactly the same. "I like what you've done with the place."

Next to me, the soul collector beamed as though I'd complimented him. "Grand, isn't it?"

"That's not what I'd say."

The sound of shuffling pulled my attention behind me. I glanced over my shoulder and flinched.

I knew I was in the in-between, the same pocket of reality where I'd spent time with my gran. Only instead of it being crowded with recently deceased mortals' souls, it was packed with animals.

A golden retriever wagged its tail when my eyes traveled over it. Sitting next to it was a large German shepherd with sad eyes. I spotted a few toads, some snakes, and even a green and red parrot perched with a few ravens. Four cats huddled together—two grays that could have been siblings, a longhaired orange, and one with gleaming black fur that had me do a doubletake.

I knew that cat. I'd seen him with my gran only a few days ago when he had snapped at me for nearly stepping over him on the street. But what was he doing here?

I took a step forward and said, "Hildo?"

9

The cat's, or rather, the familiar's yellow eyes widened at the sound of his name. "You know me? I don't recognize you." His voice was deeper than I remembered but still young-sounding. He sat back on his haunches as his tail whipped behind him, and his eyes focused like he was trying to see if I was friend or foe.

"Well, not exactly," I told him, aware that I had the undivided attention of all the other animal familiars as well. "But I did... uh... bump into you in the street a few days ago. I was with my grandmother, Eleanor Davenport."

The cat's ears swiveled on his head. "You're Eleanor's granddaughter? So, you're a witch?"

"I am."

Hildo jumped to his feet and padded over to

me until he was right at my feet. "I vaguely remember someone nearly running me over, but I remember them being big and hairy. That was you?"

Big and hairy? I raised a brow. "Running over is a bit exaggerated."

"Squishing? Flattening? Crushing? I can keep going. I've been known as the cat who never shuts up."

I laughed. "You're a handful. Aren't you?" I liked him immediately.

The cat flashed his pointy teeth, and I realized it was his way of smiling, which could have been construed as creepy. "You better believe it."

His short black fur was silky and smooth—a far cry from the rotten flesh with clumps of fur and see-through holes that had shown his bones the last time we'd met. In the in-between, he was healthy and fit with long legs and an equally long tail. He was glorious, and for a moment I was tempted to pick him up, but I wasn't sure he'd like that. I had to remember I wasn't looking at a living cat familiar. I was staring at his soul, a representation of what he was when he was alive.

I'd always wanted a familiar, probably since I realized they were real, which was around the age of five. But, as we all know how the story goes, my mother wouldn't hear of it. Imagine my utter disappointment when I learned that not one of my three aunts had an animal companion.

Perhaps, when this was all over, I'd fetch me a familiar.

I stared at the familiars, a sinking feeling in my gut. "What are you all doing here?" I'd always wondered what happened to the dead pet familiars that had risen with the dead residents of Hollow Cove Cemetery. I'd imagined they'd all gone back to their graves with their witch companions. By the looks of it, they were *all* here, trapped in the in-between. But why? Something didn't feel right.

Hildo watched me for a long moment, but the cat didn't answer. Instead, his yellow eyes flicked to my left.

"Tessa." The soul collector was suddenly next to me, a briefcase in his hand. That's when I realized I no longer had mine. "Janet's soul is ready to be processed." He gestured with his briefcase to something behind me. Not something, someone.

I whirled around. Janet stood in her light blue hospital gown. She looked up at me, and though her features were calm and smooth, I could see fear in her eyes.

I had no idea what *processed* meant, but I knew it was bad. "How does..." My throat closed up and I couldn't finish. Knowing I still had nearly a month left of this nightmare, I didn't think I could go through with it, but I had to.

I heard an echoing thud as Jack discarded his briefcase on the floor next to him. From inside his jacket, he produced what looked like a portable cash register the size of his hand. I knew what that was.

A click was followed by the sound of printing, and finally, a small piece of paper slipped out from the bottom of the contraption.

"Janet Purcell, here's your ticket," proclaimed the soul collector as he ripped off the slip of paper and handed it to her.

Janet took it without complaint. Her pale hand twisted as she stared at the tiny piece of paper. The look on her face said it all. She was defeated. I also saw acceptance. She had made a deal with the demon and now he was here to collect her soul. She surrendered to it.

I couldn't help but feel sad and angry for Janet. In a way, she reminded me of my grandmother. Perhaps only in age, but I felt an overwhelming need to protect her and help her out of this place.

But I knew I couldn't.

For a human, Janet was taking it all extremely well. I guessed she'd had years to prepare herself for this day. Still, if this were me, I'd fight the demon with everything I had. I'd never let him take me without a fight. But this wasn't about me.

"Follow me, please," said the soul collector as he turned on his heel and started forward into the darkness.

I shifted nervously, not for me, but for Janet. I knew I would hate what was going to happen next.

I followed Jack, as he made his way further into the darkness. Janet never said a word, not a single one as she followed. The feeling of dread rolled in the pit of my stomach, making me nauseated and threatening Marcus's dinner to make a comeback.

I couldn't see anything beyond the darkness, yet Jack seemed to know where he was going.

A moment later, the demon snapped his fingers and a cloud of darkness lifted, like a gust of wind pushing out the fog. The darkness rolled back until I could see a shape. I stared at a metal contraption with knobs and buttons, the size of ten refrigerators pushed together.

Jack pointed to a small opening on the machine. "Your ticket in the slot, if you please, Janet."

Janet did as she was told and slid her ticket into a slit. After some grinding metal sounds, red lights flared to life, and then a compartment opened with a clunk.

It reminded me of the containment unit for the permanent storage of ghosts used in the *Ghostbusters* movies. Only this one was for the permanent storage of souls until they were traded or ingested.

When my eyes found Janet again, my throat throbbed. "What's going to happen to Janet? Is this—"

Janet's body began to shimmer until I could see right through her to the metal contraption behind her. I could see that she still held on to her fear. Then her body, her soul, collapsed into a single see-through string that twirled and then slid into the opened slot.

With his hand, Jack shut the compartment. "And there you have it. Your first soul collection and processing. That wasn't so hard. Now, was it?"

The ground wavered at my feet. I felt disgusted and ashamed. I took a deep breath, feeling like I was becoming one of them. Becoming a soul collector...

"He got your soul too, huh? What'd you ask for?"

I looked down to find Hildo at my feet. He was the only familiar brave enough to have followed. "Money? Fame?" continued the cat. "Let me guess... the big L.O.V.E. Yeah. You look like a sucker for love. L'amour, toujours, l'amour."

I shook my head, struggling to find my voice again. "He didn't take my soul."

"He didn't?" The cat cocked its head, his yellow eyes round and unblinking. "I don't get it. Then why are you here?"

"It's a long story," I answered, though I knew I

could probably tell it in a few seconds. Maybe I just didn't want to at this very moment.

"She works for me." The soul collector pressed a few buttons on the soul containment machine, seemingly pleased with himself. He turned around and said, "Tessa is my... assistant, if you will. My soul collector in training."

"What?" growled the cat. "You're a goddamn soul collector? You steal souls from witches and familiars to take us here? To this place? To trap us in this machine? To kill our souls? But you're a witch? How could you do that?"

I knelt to be able to speak to Hildo at eye level. "Listen. It's not what he says. Well, kinda. But it's not." I shook my head. "I'm not making any sense. Look, I didn't have a choice."

Ears back, the cat hissed at me. "I thought you were a friend," he spat, his black fur bristling, "but you're one of them."

"I am! I mean, I'm *not* like him. I'm a friend." The more I opened my mouth, the worse it got.

Hildo eyed me, which was more like a frown, and then he bounded away and ran up to the other familiars that were still in the exact spot I'd seen them last. The hushed voices that raised in tempo a few seconds later were enough to know that they all thought I was a soul collector. Maybe I was.

I stood up, anger rippling out of me. "You didn't have to do that," I ground out, my jaw clenching.

"Do what?" Jack had the nerve to look innocent. "Tell the truth? You are what I say you are. You are in my servitude. Therefore, you *are* a soul collector."

I was going to punch him in the face. "You're an asshole."

Jack shook his head at me. "Temper, temper. Don't pretend to be something you're not. You collect souls. That makes you a soul collector. Just like me."

"I'm nothing like you," I snapped, but the words felt feeble on my lips. "Only until my time's up. And then I hope to never see you ever again for as long as I live."

Jack's body stiffened as he pulled out his pocket watch. He mumbled a few words I couldn't catch. "... not enough. Still not enough. Running out of time..."

He started to pace, unintelligible words continuing to spill out of his mouth. He looked more out of control than the time I'd refused my ticket. What was up with that?

My gaze shot to his soul containment machine and back to him. "You're running out of time? Why? What's going on? What are you not telling me?" I knew I had no business asking, and that he'd probably never tell me, but I couldn't help myself. As I said before, I was a curious beast.

When Jack glanced over to me, he looked like he just realized he'd said too much. Then his face became stiff as he carefully reeled in his emotions.

"You should go. You'll need your rest. Tomorrow night is a big night for you," he said calmly. One hand resting on his hip and the other cupping his chin, he eyed me speculatively.

"Why do I get the feeling I'm going to hate it more than I did tonight."

"Lots of souls to collect."

The sound of a cat hissing pulled my attention back to the crowd of familiars. I found Hildo staring at me again like he wanted nothing more than to scratch my eyes out. I still thought he was cute, though, and I didn't blame him. I hated me too at the moment.

Yet...

"Why are the familiars here?" I yanked my gaze back on the demon. "I don't remember hearing about them. They weren't in the contract you had with Craig Lancaster. Were they?" I wasn't sure, but I was betting I was right.

Jack pressed his thin lips together and said, "The witch companions share a bond with their witch. They share power through their souls, their energy. That shared power becomes a unit. The witch's soul and their familiar are one. When I collected the souls, if a familiar was attached to that soul, well, they came too." He laughed. "Two for one. Isn't that what you mortals call a sweet deal?"

I glowered at the demon. "It isn't right."

Jack watched me for a moment, emotions flickering over him. "It is what it is."

I glanced back at the familiars. Hildo had stepped a little closer, his head cocked to the side with his ears swiveling like he was listening to our conversation. "They weren't here when I was with Gran."

"No. They materialized soon after you and your father left. That happens sometimes with witch companions. First the witch and then the companion."

I narrowed my eyes. "So then why didn't they return to their graves with their witches? We made a deal. My services for their souls."

"It's complicated."

I crossed my arms over my chest and gave Jack my own signature frown. I took pointers from my Gran. "If I'm to be in your servitude for a while, I demand to know."

"You demand?" laughed Jack. "You'll get what I want to give. Nothing more. Nothing less."

But I wasn't giving up. "Why are their souls still here? What trick did you pull to keep them?"

"Their souls." He gestured to the familiars. "Were not specified in the contract you signed. Just the souls contracted by Craig Lancaster. There was no mention to add the familiar souls to that contract. There is no reason for me to give them back."

I stared at the hairless, white-eyed demon. The thought of Jack taking the familiars' souls made my anger rise tenfold. He took them when they weren't his to take. "What happens to them now?" I asked, seeing as he hadn't transferred them to the soul containment machine.

Jack smiled at me. "I haven't decided yet. Time for you to go." Yeah, he was lying. He stepped toward me and I cringed inwardly, knowing he was about to send me back.

I might be leaving, but I knew I'd be back. I also knew I wasn't about to let Hildo and the other familiars rot in the in-between. Their souls weren't for Jack. They weren't for anyone.

And I was going to figure out how to set them free.

10

It had been a little over two weeks since I'd accepted the soul collector's deal, and every afternoon I woke to the same aches and pains, feeling like I was losing myself. And every day it had gotten worse.

It was my thirtieth birthday today. It might as well have been my fiftieth, the way I was feeling. Maybe even my sixtieth. Every muscle, bone, skin, hair, and cell in my body hurt. Everything hurt. If it was on me or part of me, it hurt.

No matter if Jack had given me his super suit that enabled me to world-jump, the fact remained, my body wasn't meant to travel through other planes of reality, other worlds, other dimensions. And it was taking a toll on me.

Groaning, I pressed a hand to my head, where a

monumental headache was knocking just above my eyes. I shivered slightly at an oncoming fever.

Great. That's all I needed today. "Nothing Ruth's cooking won't cure," I said, my voice sounding haggard and low. I grimaced as my breath came back to me. It was vile, like something had died in my throat. Yeah, I was definitely coming down with something.

On any other day, I would have probably stayed in bed. But not today.

Marcus had texted me last night that he had a "special" dinner planned for my birthday. Not taking any chances this time of another Allison ambush (though Grace really had been ill from inhaling all that bleach) Marcus had told me he'd made reservations somewhere secret and hinted at a surprise rendezvous afterward. The thought of Marcus's glorious, golden body on top of me was the only thing that coaxed me to get out of bed.

We'd been missing each other for weeks. Him because of his work, and the same with me. I would wake up late in the afternoon, moody and tired. Having to scam the souls of mortals would do that to a person. I was mentally and physically exhausted.

With a moan, I swung my legs off of my bed and waited a few beats for the dizziness to subside somewhat. When I stood, I heard the bones in my knees and ankles pop and crack as I felt my muscles pull and protest. "Damn. I need a vacation."

Not bothering to turn on the lights or glance at myself in the mirror, I peed, brushed my teeth, pulled on a comfy blue sweater paired with some gray sweatpants, and went downstairs in search of Ruth. If I didn't get her special rejuvenating echinacea tea soon, I might have to spend the rest of the day in bed at the rate I was going. But no way was I going to miss date night with my wereape.

When I finally made it to the bottom of the stairs, I could hear a faucet running in the background and a hiss of something cooking in the kitchen. Then the soft clink of glasses and the loud racket of conversation intruded. I inhaled the scent of French toast with cinnamon. Before leaving for my "night job" last night, Ruth had asked me what I wanted to eat when I woke up today. Since it was my birthday, she wanted to make something special. She looked so utterly happy at the prospect I didn't have the heart to tell her that every day she made something special. She was just that good of a person. I loved my little Ruthy.

"How do I look?" I heard Beverly say as I neared the kitchen. She stood with one hand on her hip as she traced the curves of her lowcut fuchsia blouse with the other. Her dark skinny jeans looked painted on. No way you could pull those up without some magic. She'd finished her look with a pair of black suede ankle boots. No one could deny she was beautiful.

"Like a horny slut," offered Dolores.

Except for my Aunt Dolores.

Beverly smiled at her sister and cocked her hip. "There's nothing wrong with being horny. I am horny. So horny, I'm breaking into hives. Good thing Antonio's coming to pick me up in an hour. I don't think I can keep these lustful, overpowering, bodily sensations inside much longer," she complained dramatically. "The man can do wonders with his hands... and his—"

"Okay. I've heard enough." I laughed as I walked in. "We get the picture."

And then a few things happened at once.

"Ahhh!" howled Beverly.

"Ahh!" screeched Dolores at the top of her lungs.

"Ah!" I screamed because, well, they started it.

I blinked at them, confused. "Uh... why are we screaming?"

Beverly froze, looking at me like I'd just sprouted a third arm from my forehead, while Dolores stiffened in her seat at the kitchen table. Her mouth twitched like it had a mind of its own as she fought to control it.

"Cauldron help us," Dolores said finally with the same crazed look shared by her sister.

At that moment, Ruth turned around. "Happy—holy cannoli!" she screeched, and dropped the pot she was holding, spilling cream-colored batter all over her bare feet.

They were all gawking at me with shocked expressions, kind of like how they'd stared at Gran when she'd popped into the kitchen a few weeks ago.

Okay, now I was feeling a little self-conscious. "Right. I confess. I haven't taken a shower yet." I chuckled, not appreciating how their eyes kept getting wider the longer I stood there feeling like a new species at the zoo. "I promise once I have something to eat, I'll go wash my dirty ass. I just... I just don't feel so great."

"You don't look so great." Beverly's eyes were wide in question, her pretty mouth pinched in what could only be horror.

"Thanks. A bit rude, even for you," I told her, feeling heat rise to my face though I wasn't sure if it was from a sudden burst of anger or the fever. Maybe both. "I'm tired. I was up all night... working." I wasn't in the mood to talk about my soul-collecting job. It was hard enough that I had to do it. No need to add insult to injury. I felt injured enough. Thank you very much.

"No, you don't understand." Dolores slowly stood up from the kitchen table, her face pale. Her expression was twisted up in shock and surprise. "You don't look like... yourself. Well, you do look like yourself..."

"Only different," finished Ruth, as she shifted her weight from foot to foot as though she had to pee. "A lot different. Really, really different."

"Your vocabulary keeps improving in leaps and bounds," scoffed Dolores.

I glanced around at the stunned expressions mirrored on every aunt. "What? I'm tired. And I think I'm coming down with something." I put a hand on my forehead, feeling it warm, and looked at Ruth. "Ruth. Can you make me some of that echinacea tea?"

Beverly waved her red manicured fingers in my direction. "You're going to need something stronger than tea to cover up that mess."

I frowned, feeling too exhausted and ill to get into a fight with them. "What's the matter with all of you? And why are you all staring at me like I just stepped off of the train from Mars?"

"Because that's exactly what it looks like," commented Dolores, worry lines creasing her forehead.

Tension pulled my shoulders at the concern I saw in her dark eyes. I shook my head. "What?" When they didn't answer I shouted, "What!" And then I immediately regretted it as it escalated the pounding in my head. All I wanted now was my bed, but I didn't think I could climb up all those stairs.

The aunts shared a look that I didn't like.

Finally, Dolores cleared her throat. "You've... *aged* a bit."

Beverly snorted. "Aged a bit? She looks like she's from the Middle Ages."

I stilled. "What do you mean?" Pulse pounding, I looked around the kitchen for a mirror, anything. I grabbed the toaster, pulled it to my face, and stared at my reflection.

And then...

I screamed like the queen of all banshees.

My long tresses of brown hair were brittle and gray, mixed with strands of white. The face that stared back at me was thin, drawn, and peppered with age spots. Loose skin drooped around my neck and mouth, and my cheeks were down somewhere around my jaw line. My eyes were watery and looked kind of sad at the moment. And I was wrinkled like a walnut.

I blinked at the person reflected in the toaster. It was the face of a haggard old woman, withered and brownish, surrounded by wispy white and gray hair.

It wasn't me. It couldn't be me. Could it?

"What the hell is this?" I shrieked and dropped the toaster. I whirled to my aunts. "I—I—I look old! I look like you!"

Yeah, not the best thing to say to a group of middle-aged women, but the words just flew out of my mouth.

Beverly glared at me, her hands on her hips. "Who are you calling old? You look older than us, darling. Like you're pushing eighty. I don't look a day over forty."

Dolores snorted. "In what calendar year? The Mayans'?"

Beverly shot her sister a venomous look under her perfect makeup.

I pressed my hands to my face, feeling for the first time how alien it felt with the dry and soft leathery wrinkles. My skin had always been oily. I rolled a long strand of white hair between my shaking fingers. I wasn't a vain person, but I did care about how I looked to a certain extent. But this? This... I wasn't prepared for this.

I had a few moments of denial, even a burst of nervous giggles, but then the reality of the situation hit. It explained why I felt this way—bent, frail, and tired. It was like I was trapped in the body of an eighty-year-old woman like my life had skipped fifty years while I'd slept.

I stared at my hands, spotted with large veins and knuckles like knobs. The gnarled hands belonged to an older woman with severe arthritis, but they were my hands. I shook with a combination of horror and panic. The kitchen suddenly felt too small, and I couldn't get enough air into my lungs. Oh, yeah. I was having a meltdown.

The room started to spin. "I need to sit down," I said weakly, as I started to tip forward.

Ruth rushed over, her toes making batter toeprints on the wood floors as she grabbed me by the shoulders and held me up. "Here. Come sit over here."

I let Ruth guide me to a chair like I was her elderly sister who'd forgotten her walker. I don't think I would have made it without her help. I could barely feel my legs.

"Now," said Ruth as she leaned back. "Don't you worry. I'll have that echinacea tea for you in a jiffy. We'll figure this out. Just sit there and don't move."

"Where do you think she's going to go?" Dolores gave a harsh laugh. "She can't go anywhere looking like that. She looks like one of the witches from Macbeth."

Ruth glared at her sister but kept her mouth shut as she picked up the pot from the floor, dropped it in the kitchen sink, and grabbed a new pot. She filled it with water and set it on the stove before she started sprinkling herbs in it.

I stared at my hands again. I couldn't help it. They looked alien to me, like I was wearing someone else's skin over mine.

I pressed them to my throat. "My voice."

"Is different too," answered Dolores. "It aged. Like the rest of you."

I looked at the pain reflecting in her eyes. "I'm not afraid of growing old. If that's what you think."

"Speak for yourself," huffed Beverly, watching me with a weird kind of intensity while keeping her distance as though what made me age was perhaps contagious.

I swallowed hard. "I just wanted to grow old at a normal pace, so I could get used to the changes. But this..." It was unfair. That's what that was. How could this have happened?

Dolores put a hand on my shoulder. "Don't overexert yourself now. We'll figure this out."

My horror turned to confusion. "I don't understand this. I looked fine yesterday. Well, maybe that's an exaggeration. I was tired, but I still looked like me. Like a thirty-year-old woman. I didn't look like... this."

"You're still you," said Beverly, a forced smile on her pretty face. "Just older. You've aged at least fifty years. Maybe more."

I shook my head. "But how? Why?" Why had this happened to me? The only explanation for an overnight transformation of this magnitude was... someone had cursed me.

Steaming with anger, I shifted in my chair. "Allison," I hissed her name like it was poison on my lips. "She did this. She cursed me." With my anger came a sudden relief. Curses could be reversed. If Allison had cursed me, my aunts could come up with a counterspell and I'd be me again in no time.

Dolores watched me. "Allison isn't skilled in magic. There's no way she could have done this."

"Then she paid someone to do it for her. It's her revenge because of Iris's curse." It all made perfect sense.

Dolores raised her hand. "Wait a minute. Iris cursed Allison? Why?"

"Good." Beverly curled a lock of hair behind her head. "About time someone did. People that good-looking shouldn't be allowed to exist."

Dolores was shaking her head, her brows low at the bridge of her nose. "It's not a curse, Tessa. I'm not getting any residual energies that come with the use of curses and hexes or any kind of magical activity. This isn't magic."

My little hope bubble burst, but I wasn't completely convinced. "If this isn't magic, what is it? What else can explain what happened to me?"

With a coffee in her hand, Dolores pulled the chair next to me and sat. "I know why. It's that deal you made with the soul collector. Our bodies aren't meant to go back and forth to those places." She leaned forward until her elbows rested on the table.

"I don't know why it only showed up now after weeks of doing it, but somehow traveling through those other worlds sped up the aging process."

"But I'm part demon," I disagreed. "Surely my body could handle it better. Right?" But even as the words left me, I knew she was right. I'd felt it the very first time when I came back home. My body had weakened.

"Apparently not," countered Dolores. "You might have a demon father, but I'm willing to bet you've got a lot more witch in you."

I had a sinking feeling in my gut. "Does that mean another few weeks of this and I'll be a hundred? Then what? I'm not immortal. This is going to kill me." Did Jack know this was going to happen to me? Why hadn't he told me?

"We won't let that happen." Ruth put a large, steaming mug in front of me. "Drink up. All of it, please. I'll make you that French toast I promised for your birthday."

Beverly widened her eyes. "Worst birthday ever. You missed decades of them."

"Not helping, Beverly," growled Dolores.

I stared at the mug. I'd be a fool not to listen to Ruth. "I'll drink the tea, but I don't think I can eat." I jerked in my seat. "Oh, my god. Marcus!"

"Marcus!" Ruth spun around like a top with a

spoon in her hand, a happy smile on her face as she stared at the back door, expecting him to emerge.

"He's not here, you nitwit," snapped Dolores.

"He can't see me like this." Maybe I was a bit vain. The chief had been used to seeing a thirty-year-old. I didn't want to see the shock on his face when he saw this.

Crap. If my face looked like the face of an eighty-year-old woman... what did that do to the rest of me?

Grabbing the collar of my sweater, I pulled it away from my chest and looked down at what was supposed to be my breasts.

"What the hell are those?" I wailed, letting go of my sweater.

"Granny titties," expressed Beverly, making Dolores choke on her coffee. "It's a slippery slope from there on, darling. Don't worry. I've got some fabulous push-up bras that will bring the old girls right up."

I wanted to die.

I let my head fall on the kitchen table. "I can't let Marcus see me like this." He'll run away and never look back. The only person who would be ecstatic to see me like this was Allison. Yeah, better not let her see me either.

"And he won't," promised Dolores. "We'll keep him away."

"But he has this thing planned for my birthday tonight."

"We'll figure something out."

I lifted my head and met Dolores's eyes. "I will be normal again. Right? This is just a temporary glitch? If I stop working for the soul collector, my body will spring back to what it was. Right?"

Dolores just stared at me, the emotions running across her face. I knew she was struggling with what to say next. It was written all over her face, though she didn't even need to say it. She had no idea.

Ruth came over and tapped my hand. "Don't you worry. You have enough to worry about with that new job. Give me a few hours and I'll whip up a potion to reverse the aging process. Finish the tea, please."

I took a big gulp of Ruth's tea and immediately felt less pressure behind my eyes as my fever lifted. But when I looked back at my hands, they were still spotted with my knuckles swollen. "You have something like that?" I glanced at Beverly, doubtful. "If you had a potion to magic a few facelifts, I'm surprised you haven't tried it."

Beverly frowned at me. "What are you saying? That I look my age?" She seemed angry.

"No, it's just..." yeah, maybe a little.

"They don't last," informed Dolores. "And sometimes, the effects of the elixir are not what you were expecting."

"They can make it worse," offered Beverly.

My heart fell to the bottom of my gut. "Worse? Worse than looking eighty instead of thirty?"

Ruth huffed angrily. "Would you two stop? You're scaring her."

"She should be scared," answered Beverly.

I pulled my eyes away from Aunt Beverly before I lost it. I knew this was bad, but if I had known being in the service of the soul demon meant I'd age like this, I wouldn't have accepted.

I took another sip of my tea. I heard a plop, and when I glanced at the cup something small had fallen inside it. Ignoring the hot tea, I plunged in my gnarled hands to retrieve a small yellow tooth. "Great. I'm losing my teeth."

"Oh! Give it here." Ruth snatched up my tooth, smiling. "I'll put it under your pillow for the Tooth Faery."

Dolores smacked her forehead. "And we let her cook for us."

I took a deep breath. My stomach roiled at the look of defeat my aunts shared. They didn't believe their magic could help me because this was something different. If this was demonic magic or whatever, then following that logic, I needed demon magic to reverse what happened.

I jolted in my seat. "I know who can help me," I said suddenly, wanting to kick myself for not thinking of it sooner.

"Who?" asked Dolores, as both Beverly and Ruth homed their full attention on me.

"Obi-Wan Kenobi." I smiled and said, "My father."

11

What does a thirty-year-old woman in an eighty-year-old body do to pass the time?

One word—Spanx.

Lots and lots of Spanx.

"I can't pull it any higher," I said, yanking the cream-colored bodysuit as hard as I could. "Any higher than that, and my breasts are going to say hello to my chin."

"I think we're done." Iris took a step back, admiring her handiwork—literally. She'd spent a half-hour just trying to pull the Spanx over my thighs and hips. My eighty-year-old body wasn't as flexible as it used to be. Plus, it was really hard to yank spandex material over loose skin.

I'd texted Iris a 9-1-1 after I'd downed another one of Ruth's echinacea teas, which actually worked wonders to eradicate my fever completely and make me feel better. I'd asked her to buy all the Spanx shapewear she could get her hands on in Hollow Cove.

I stared at all the unopened packages of booty boost leggings, high-waisted mid-thigh shorts, bodysuits, high power panties, and push-up bras, all spread out on my bed. "Where'd you find all these?"

"Martha sells them at her salon," answered the Dark witch. "I took everything she had. She kept asking why I needed them all."

"What did you tell her?" I knew if Martha got wind of what had happened to me, the entire town would know in a matter of hours. That included Marcus.

"That I had a wedding to go to and I still hadn't picked the dress," she answered as I let out a sigh of relief. Iris gestured with her hand. "Come take a look."

I moved to the mirror over my dresser and stared at the old lady looking back. The cream-colored Spanx started just above my knee, which was covered in folds of loose skin, and stretched to my breasts like a one-piece bathing suit. Though I didn't know of any bathing suits with a secret opening for when nature called.

"I've been Spanxed."

Iris choked on a laugh. Eyes wide, she said, "I'm sorry. I didn't mean to laugh."

I pulled my hair back into a low bun. "It's fine. I'd be laughing too if I wasn't so depressed." I lifted my arms to the sides and made circles, watching as the sagging meat of skin and muscle rocked back and forth. "Look. I can wave at you without even using my hands." I laughed, trying hard not to cry.

Iris forced a smile. "Ruth will find something," she said, worry etching her brow.

A knock came from my door. "Can I come in now?" whined Ronin from outside my bedroom door. "I've been standing out here for hours. Iris said you might have been cursed. I want to see."

I raised a brow. "Are half-vampires always such babies?"

Iris shrugged. "No idea, but men are."

I turned and spoke to the door. "If you laugh, Ronin, I'm going to castrate you. No joke."

There was a loud sigh. "What am I? Twelve? I'm a grown-ass man." When I said nothing, he added, "I promise I won't laugh. Now, let me in, or I'm going to kick this door down."

Iris snorted. "I'd like to see that." Her smile was infectious, and on another day I would have loved to join her. But I found I couldn't.

Apart from my aunts and Marcus, Iris and Ronin were the only people I trusted. He sounded genuinely worried. Though knowing him, I figured Ronin might laugh, but I'd get over it because I knew he had my back.

"Just a sec," I called out and moved to my bed, slower than I was used to since my body was stiffer than I remembered. I pulled on the same pair of sweatpants from before because, let's face it, nothing else fit. But this time I matched it with a navy hoodie.

Once I was done, I gave a nod to Iris and she pulled open the door.

Ronin strode inside, his eyes everywhere at once until they settled on me. He froze, his eyes widening the longer he looked at me, and his lips parted in soundless words. His usual confident, sly expression quickly morphed into something like horror and then pity, as though I'd just told him I had incurable cancer.

The half-vampire was silent. The fact that he didn't laugh or make a joke made me feel worse. A hell of a lot worse. Like it made it permanent somehow.

Ronin raked his fingers through his brown hair. I watched as he tried to hide the visible worry and tension in his body. It didn't work.

Iris must have seen something on my face because she smacked Ronin hard on the arm. "Stop staring at her like that." She frowned at him in a way that suggested she'd warned him about me earlier.

Ronin rubbed his arm. "Sorry. This is... it's just not what I was expecting," he said, trying to hide his concern with a tight smile. I found my eyes burning at his words.

When Iris had brought me the Spanx earlier, she'd been shocked at first, but then she had quickly recovered as she went to work to help me Spanx myself. Yeah, I knew how that sounded.

I pulled the hoodie over my head. "Imagine *my* surprise."

Ronin took a step closer, seemingly having gotten over the initial shock. He dipped his head as his eyes rolled over my face, my head, all the way to my feet, inspecting me like I was a new magical creature. "You shrank. Like a good three inches."

"I can always count on you for flattery."

The half-vampire shrugged. "We all know when we age we shrink a bit. Gravity's a bitch." Moving to one of my chairs, he let himself fall in it, stretched out, and crossed his ankles.

I glared at the half-vampire, doubting that gravity would ever affect him. He'd probably look this good for another hundred years. Damn those vampire genes.

Ronin folded his hands on his thighs. "But this *is* a curse. Right? Curses can be reversed. I'm surprised you're wasting your time playing dress-up and not working on a reversal right now."

I looked over to Iris before answering. "It's not a curse. I thought it was. I thought Allison was getting back at me, but my aunts confirmed it's not."

Ronin looked at Iris, who nodded her head. "She's right. It's not a curse. I did a revealing spell just before. There's no magical residue. No traces. Nothing."

"So what do you think this is?"

I told him what Dolores had concluded. "I think she's right. I started to feel strange after my first night. And then after every night, it got worse, but I never noticed anything different about my appearance until this afternoon."

Ronin leaned forward, resting his elbows on his thighs. "So this deal you made to save your gran's soul is slowly turning you into Granny Tess?"

"Ironic. Isn't it?" I answered, staring at the suit I'd carefully draped over my other chair. "It has something to do with me, with my body, physically being pulled or whatever happens when I travel back and forth between worlds."

Ronin flashed me a smile. "You might be Granny Tess, but you're still hot."

I laughed, feeling some of my pent-up tension leave my stiff shoulders. "You know... you're one sick puppy, but I love you anyway."

"All the ladies love me, even the old-timers." Ronin smirked.

"Urgh." Iris rolled her eyes and looked over at me. "Have you met anyone so in love with himself before?"

"Every time I look in the mirror, baby," answered Ronin.

I cackled, actually cackled. The sound surprised me coming out of my mouth, but then it gave way to another cackle. I sounded like... I sounded like my gran. If she was here now, we could have been twinzies.

I was grateful to have some amazing and loving friends. They'd dropped everything to come to me. That was true friendship.

I sat on my bed and began the exercise routine of pulling on my socks. Beads of sweat formed on my forehead. Who knew it would be such a workout?

"You know," I said, breathing hard, "the one thing that could have been really awesome with this transformation would have been the wisdom that came with it. The magical knowledge. Imagine what I could do with fifty-plus years of knowledge?"

"Beat me at Scrabble?" laughed Ronin. Seeing his stupid smiling face made me laugh too.

"What about Marcus?" Iris sat at the edge of the bed next to me.

I lost my smile. "What about him?"

Iris gave me a pointed look. "He doesn't know. Does he?"

Ronin whistled. "Can I be here when you tell him? Or is it *show* him?"

I tried to stand, but my ass seemed to be stuck to my bed. I rocked for a bit until I had enough forward momentum to propel myself up. "He doesn't know. And that's how it's going to stay."

"He's going to find out." Iris leaned back. At my frown, she added. "He's the chief. The chief always knows. Why wouldn't you tell him? I thought the two of you were getting close."

"We are."

Iris pinched her face in thought. "Don't you have that *thing* tonight?"

"What thing?" asked Ronin, his eyes flicking from me to Iris. "There's a thing I don't know about?"

I looked up and glanced at myself in the mirror, temporarily having forgotten the old lady who lived there and flinched. "It's no big deal. Just, Marcus was taking me out for my birthday."

"Just tell him," said Ronin. "The guy's decent. He'll understand."

"Because I don't want him to see me like this," I said before I could control myself and the emotions in my voice. "Maybe I'm vain. Maybe my looks are more important than I thought." Maybe because a certain gorgeous blonde is still in town. "Either way, if my father can fix me, what's the point? He doesn't have to see me like this."

"Are you sure he can?" asked Iris. "I mean, you don't know for sure, though. Right?"

"He can," I said, sounding like I was trying to convince myself. "It's time. Come on."

Not waiting for them to answer—not because I didn't want to talk about it but because I knew it would take me twice as long to go down the stairs as it normally did—I left my room and headed toward the staircase. My body was slightly bent but not overly so. My legs might not be thirty-year-old legs, but they were still strong, albeit a little stiff.

And like any smart eighty-year-old woman, I made sure to hold on to the railing and took my freaking time going down the stairs.

After what felt like half an hour later, I made it to the bottom of the stairs and shuffled toward the entrance with Ronin at my elbow, just in case I fell or tripped. Iris rushed to the small entryway closet to fetch my coat.

"I could get used to this." My voice cracked in laughter.

"Not funny." Iris slipped my arms through my coat sleeves and pulled it over my shoulders before tugging down the sleeves.

"Oh! Tessa," called Ruth from the kitchen, and I shuffled forward down the hallway until I could see a worried Dolores sitting at the table with her reading glasses going through a book that looked just as old as me. "What time will you be back?"

"I don't know," I told her. "Why? What are you making?"

Ruth's face brightened at my question. "The elixir of youth. I still need about two hours for the spell to hold, but it'll work. Not that your idea won't," she added quickly, seeing something on my face. "This is just a precaution. Just in case."

"Thanks."

"It's not a cure, but it should rejuvenate your body and reverse the signs of premature aging. Like a nip and tuck." She chuckled and slashed her wooden spoon in the air like she was slicing through meat or something. "Think of me as your plastic surgeon with a scalpel."

"No idiot doctor would give you a scalpel," snapped Dolores. "Not even if he was Dr. Frankenstein."

Ruth's smile never wavered. "I'll see you when you get back."

I turned and waddled back to the entrance, reaching out and feeling the pulsing energy of the ley line. I let out a breath of relief. Thank the cauldron I could still tap into the ley lines.

"You're really sure he can fix you?" Iris's face had gone all serious again, making me doubt myself.

I stared at Iris, trying to keep the frustration from my face. "This," I gestured to my body, "is demon magic. If anyone can fix me, it's him."

I reached out, grabbed the door handle, and pulled open the door. Cold, icy, January wind tugged at my hair and coat, and I felt cold despite the layers I had on.

Steeling myself, I focused my will and felt the ley line's magic in my mind, flowing by with a power that pulsated up through the soles of my boots.

Iris gaped at me. Worry had drawn her face into lines. "But what if he can't help?"

I pulled my eyes from my friends. "That's not an option," I said, and then I jumped.

12

I soared into the ley line like a cannon ball. Images sped by, blurred and barely recognizable as I raced forward in the ley line through a wail of wind and colors.

But riding the ley lines as an eighty-year-old woman had its challenges.

I screamed and then peed a little (an eighty-year-old bladder is not the same as a thirty-year-old one) as the force of the ley line pushed me back until I was nearly horizontal. Arms out, I strained to pull myself forward, but it was like riding a jet with five G's, and gravity kept pushing me back. My older body lacked the core muscles necessary to pull myself up.

Shit. I hadn't thought this through.

If I didn't do something quickly, I would be yanked out of the ley line at the speed of light. And if I hit a wall, a house, or even a car, nothing would be left of me. There was also the more plausible outcome of being yanked out in pieces—my legs plopped on the sidewalk in Maine while my torso rolled down a hill in Greenland.

Panic set in as I felt myself losing control, my grip on the ley line's power failing. I had to do something quickly or being trapped in an eighty-year-old body was the least of my problems.

Crap! This wasn't supposed to be happening!

My breath was quick and ragged. Frightened, I grasped my will and forced myself to focus and grab hold of the ley line's terrifying power. Pain resonated through my body, my core, and I cried out. Muscles went limp, bones popped, and my cry came out as a harsh gurgle. Terror smothered me like a blanket. I was going to die.

Utter fear gave me strength. I tried to yank my body forward, but it was useless. I barely had enough control to keep my body from being ejected.

My pulse hammering, the fear of dying overtook me.

And then I realized I didn't need to pull myself up to get control of the ley line. I just needed to bend it to get my father's attention.

And yeah, then pray to the cauldron he was paying attention.

Energy rushed through my head, my body, my nerves, everywhere. With the last bit of my will, I pulled on the ley line until I could see it clearly in my mind like a translucent river. And like an elastic band, I manipulated it. I bent it until I could feel its trembling energy beneath my feet, until I could see it race across the town to a stretch of forest.

"Any time now," I huffed, holding on desperately but feeling myself drown with every passing second.

My confidence trickled away, and then my energy failed as I let go of the ley line.

Oh. Shit.

I fell back on my butt as excruciating pain took control of every cell in my body. I was going to be obliterated into nothingness.

Just as I felt my body pulling in every direction, it stopped.

I felt a sudden release on the ley line's pull as the images around me solidified until they weren't blurred anymore, and I could make them out.

"Tessa? What happened to you? Why do you look like your grandmother?"

I blinked up to see a man with luminous silver eyes, a perfectly trimmed beard, and matching graying hair, wearing an expensive dark business suit and a crisp white shirt. He projected the image of a respectable, well-groomed businessman, or rather, businessdemon.

"Hi, Dad," I ground out, surprised it actually felt normal to say, like I'd been saying it my whole life. "Or should I call you, Obiryn?"

My father's eyes widened at the mention of his name. "I see. You've been talking to your mother about me. I'm not surprised. What *surprises* me is why you look like an old woman? Are you in disguise for a reason? Is this what the Merlins are up to now?"

I beamed at him. "It's a great story." I rolled over to my side panting, the creaking of my limbs loud in my ears. Swinging my right arm and pushing with my left arm, I tried to thrust myself to my feet but only managed to spin around and around. This was not going great at all.

Okay, this was harder than it looked. Who was I kidding? Sit-ups were not my forte even at thirty. The only time I did a sit-up, was when I had to *sit up* from my bed.

Straining, I tried to squeeze my core muscles to propel myself up, but all I managed to do was let out a ripping fart.

Whoops.

But seriously, a little more hot air might have been enough to give me a good push.

"Beans for lunch?" chuckled my father.

"Very funny." Cursing, and with great effort, I managed a sitting position and found myself out of breath. I held out a knobby hand to my father. "Can you help an old lady up?"

With his teeth showing, my father gripped my hand and carefully pulled me to my feet.

"Thanks," I said as I steadied myself, wishing I could lean on something for support until my body stopped shaking. Now I understood the necessity of Gran's cane.

I glanced around. We were in the ley line, the sound of rushing water, of power still eminent, though we were at a standstill.

My father crossed his arms over his chest, a gesture I was familiar with because he looked like me doing it. "Why do I get the impression you're about to tell me something I'm not going to like."

"Because I am." Spreading out my legs for support, I took a breath and told my father all about the deal I made with the soul collector.

"And I woke up this afternoon looking like..." I stared down at myself. "Looking like my gran. Not that I don't love the way she looked, because I do. I'm just not ready to be a senior citizen yet. I'm missing a huge gap in my life." When I looked back up at my father, his face was impassive, making it impossible to guess what he was thinking.

My father rubbed a hand over his chin. "And you have two weeks left on his service?"

I wrinkled my face in a frown. "Just about. Thirteen days. But that's not the point—"

"It is the point," said my father, his voice tinged with anger. "Even after all these years and loving a mortal witch, I still get surprised at how foolish you all can be."

I pressed my hands on my hips. "I didn't come here for you to insult me."

Eyebrows high, he said, "I saved your life from that soul collector, yet you chose to throw it away to bond yourself to him. How could you do that?"

I pursed my lips, anger bubbling up. "It was to save Gran's soul. I already told you that. And besides, you were there. You knew what he was going to do to Gran. I couldn't let that happen. You refused to help her, so I did. She's family. Where I'm from, we help our family."

My father's frown deepened until it showed on his forehead. "It's not that simple. And I don't want to get into that."

His lack of help for Gran still bothered me, but I could tell his cool composure was slipping quickly. The last thing I wanted was to argue with my newfound father. I needed him to help me, not be pissed at me.

"So," I said, letting a breath of air out and steeling my face into what I hoped was an earnest expression. I probably looked like I was passing more gas. "Can you help me? Can you reverse this demon magic so I can look like myself again?" *And be me for my hot date with the chief tonight?* If this went according to plan, my birthday was going to turn out better than I'd hoped. The thought of Marcus had tingles erupting all over my skin.

When he said nothing, I added, "It's why I came out to the ley lines to look for you. So you could help me." A tiny spark of fear kindled in my gut. "You can help me. Right? *Right?*"

My father shook his head and started to pace inside the ley line. His silver eyes looking intense, he ran his gaze over the line of trees that surrounded us on both sides. His expression was both weary and angry.

Okay, not what I was hoping for. Eyeing him warily, I asked, "What? What is it?"

When he looked back at me, lines marked his face. He looked old, and sadness flashed in his eyes. "I'm sorry, Tessa. I wish I could help you, but I can't."

My lips parted, and my heart was lodged somewhere in my throat. "I'm sorry. What?" I choked out, my knees buckling, as I could barely feel them supporting me anymore.

My father sighed. "I said—"

"I heard what you said," I snapped. "It's my freaking birthday. Can't you do this for me?"

His face went stern. "I know it is," he answered, his voice harsh. "I've missed twenty-nine of them. I wish I could give you what you want, but I can't."

"Can't or won't." I couldn't believe this guy, dad, demon, whatever. "You did it once. You saved my life. I'm going to die if you don't help me. Why wouldn't you do it again?"

Surprise, shock, and then anger cascaded over his face. His silver eyes shown with sudden brightness, and I felt myself taking a step back.

Yes, I was pissed too, but I had to remind myself that my daddy dearest was a demon, and a powerful one. Plus, I already had an estranged kind of relationship with my mother. The last thing I wanted was to push him away too. I wanted to get to know him, but if I only had a few weeks left to live, what did it matter?

I glanced around, shaking my head. "Weeks? More like days."

"Who are you talking to?" asked my father.

"My other two personalities."

Demon daddy frowned. "You shouldn't have taken that deal."

I raised a brow. "It's a little late for that. Can't you use The Force, Obi-Wan?" I asked. "Aren't you some Jedi demon knight or something?"

My father's face seemed to brighten a little. "Something like that."

"So..."

My father clasped his hands before him. "To reverse the aging that was done to you would require an enormous amount of energy. I've already used what I could on you before. I have nothing left to give."

Well, that's not good.

Okay. Trying not to panic. Trying not to panic.

Okay, plan B, which I only just thought of. "Can you at least get me out of this deal? Since... I don't know... you're Obi-Wan? The thing is, the more I jump from my world to the soul collector's, the older I get. At this rate, I'm not going to last another week." It was hard not to panic or run over there and smack him. But if Ruth could find some miraculous elixir to reverse the aging process, all I had to do was stop working for Jack. That's it. Then all would be well in my world...

"The traveling isn't what's causing your body to age so quickly," my father announced.

I had a partial brain freeze moment. And then, "It's not? I'm confused. Then why did I age? Is this a curse? A demon curse?" I didn't know any demons apart from Jack and my father, and I couldn't think up a reason why a demon would curse me.

I winced as a thought popped into my head. "Is

this because of the ley lines? Because I've been *bending* them?" Both my parents had warned me about them. Maybe the ley lines were sucking up my magical mojo like the way a vampire drains a mortal of their blood.

"Is this the 'them' my mother was speaking about?" Technically I knew she'd been referring to a group of people but maybe not.

"The *them*? What them?"

"The them that don't want me messing around with the ley lines."

My father's face seemed to take on more wrinkles, and I could see the strain his body was enduring to just stand here and talk to me. "It's the souls," he said finally. "Souls are a lifeforce, and each time you take one, it takes back."

Holy hell. I felt the blood leave my face and settle somewhere at my feet. "But Jack looks the same, and he's been taking souls for probably thousands of years."

"He's a demon. It's different."

A nauseating mix of dread and fear shook my knees, and I clamped my jaw so I wouldn't get sick. "But I'm part demon." Hey, it was worth a try.

"Which is the only reason you're still alive."

I took a shuddering breath. "But not for long." That's when my legs decided to give way.

I fell to my knees, the pain from my joints and

hip going almost unnoticed as a cry of misery escaped me. Where did I go from here? Was this the end? I'd skipped fifty years of my life only to die in a few weeks? A few days?

My father started for me, but I waved a hand.

"Don't come any closer," I warned. "I'm a fear biter."

I'd really messed things up, but I shouldn't be angry at my father. This wasn't his fault. This was all me. All of it.

But the one I could blame, the one who had purposely left this crucial part out of our deal, was the soul collector. He did this.

I ground my jaw. "Jack knew this. Didn't he? He knew by working with him I'd expire. Right?"

"Probably."

I homed in all my frustration, my fear, and it fueled me with new vigor. "I'm going to kick his ass," I muttered. "But first, I might need a hip replacement."

"Tessa, don't," warned my father.

"What? I can't get a hip replacement?"

My father rolled his eyes, actually rolled them. It was quite funny. "You're exasperating. You know that?"

I smiled. "I'm charming. Who doesn't love a wiseass old granny?" I hooked my knobby thumbs at myself.

My demon father smiled, but I saw pain mirrored in his eyes as I fastened on them, finding a calm in their silver depths. He was worried about me.

He stroked his beard. "Just... wait. Give me a few days to figure this out. Are you working tonight?"

"Unfortunately."

My father sighed through his nose. "I can teach you a glamour that will hide your *older* physical appearance." He smiled and said, "You'd be saving thousands of dollars on plastic surgery."

"But I'll still be an eighty-year-old granny. Right? I'll look thirty, but I'll be walking around with a cane?"

He just looked at me without answering. He didn't have to.

"No thanks. I'm not ashamed of being older, just pissed I didn't enjoy those years. Children? I would have loved to have them someday. I mean, who wouldn't want cute, furry, half-gorilla witch babies? But I was robbed of that choice. Robbed of all those years. He took them from me."

My father eyed me for a moment, and I could see plans formulating behind those brilliant silver eyes. "I'll see what I can do about your contract with the soul demon," said my father, though his tone said it was hopeless. "Don't do anything stupid before you hear from me."

"Me? Do something stupid? Never." All the time.

Shaking his head, he said, "You're just like me, which is why I'm worried."

"Don't be." I grinned. "Things are starting to look up. I can finally get fifty percent off on my bus pass as a senior citizen."

"This is your life we're talking about. You shouldn't be laughing."

"Why not? I won't let aging get me down. It's too damn hard getting back up." I crackled a laugh.

My father cracked a smile. "You're crazy."

"I know. Can you take me home? I don't think I can work a ley line right now. Don't think I can manage standing up either."

"I can."

A slip of energy hummed around me. The next thing I knew we were soaring again inside the ley lines. With me on my butt, it really did feel like I was driving a spaceship on hyperdrive. If I wasn't already cringing on the inside, I might have really enjoyed it.

I'm not going to lie. I was an emotional wreck. The only thing that kept my emotions glued together was my primal hatred for the soul collector.

He knew by assisting him with the souls I would eventually need a casket. He'd chosen to keep that very important detail from me.

I might be old and frail, but I wasn't dead. I still had some life in me.

Yeah, I might cry, get angry, and feel sorry for myself. But then I was going to do something about it.

And that something was... I was going to get even with Jack.

13

Having gone to see my father hadn't been a total loss. I knew now that he couldn't reverse the aging process, and that Jack was solely responsible for putting me in this old body.

But I'd also accepted it. No point in crying or drowning in self-pity. I was older. Old. And that was fine.

But I was still going to make Jack pay. Only, I hadn't figured that part out yet.

When I'd gotten home, Ruth had pulled me into the kitchen and given me a vial of purple liquid to drink—the elixir of youth.

"Here. Give it a try," she'd insisted, looking both scared and hopeful at the same time. "It should give you a few years back. Smooth out a few wrinkles." She'd winked. "Go on now, and drink it all." She rubbed her hands together, looking more anxious than I was.

Having full trust in Ruth's potion making, I chucked it down like a shot. The liquid glided down my throat like syrup, tasting of rose water, licorice, and a few herbs I couldn't recognize. I waited to feel the effects of the elixir, but all I felt was the soreness of my muscles and my aching bones.

Smacking my lips I said, "Well? Did it work? Am I me again?"

Dolores set her glass of wine on the table. "Well, if you mean do you still look like one of the witches from Macbeth? Then, yes. You still look like that."

Ruth's face was set in a deep frown. "Hmm. It should have worked. Why didn't it work? Guess this was a bad batch. Just... give me another couple of hours and I'll whip up a new one."

I'd left the kitchen feeling a little frustrated. Not because Ruth's potion didn't work but because I had to climb all those stairs to the attic.

"Why did I have to pick the room on the highest floor?"

And then something occurred to me. House was magical. I'd always thought of House as some invisible butler and in that case...

"House?" I whispered when I shuffled my way over to the staircase and out of earshot from my aunts. "Can you... pick me up and take me to my room?"

I waited but not long. A sudden rush of energy flew around me and wrapped me up like a blanket. Next, I was lifted off the ground, my knees bent as though I was sitting in an invisible chair. I felt myself relax as a bubble of energy blossomed around me.

And then I was moving.

Going up and up the staircase, I floated up to each floor, laughing in delight until I reached the platform to the attic. It occurred to me that Gran would have known about this. But I'd never seen her float up or down the stairs. The witch was too proud and stubborn to show weakness.

Me? Screw my pride. My knees were going to thank me later.

After House deposited me in front of my bedroom door, and I thanked him (him because I'd always assumed House was male) Iris and Ronin arrived moments later.

"We heard you laughing from my room," said Iris climbing up the stairs. "What's so funny?"

I shrugged. "My life."

Ronin reached the platform first. "You're still Granny Tess? Guess Daddy couldn't help."

Iris smacked his arm. "Gentle words, remember?"

"It's fine." I smiled at Iris. I knew she was worried

about my feelings, my "mental state," but I was feeling a lot better than a few hours ago.

I waved them inside and shut the door. "I did learn a few things." I quickly told them what I'd discovered about the souls and how taking them had done this to me.

"Jack's a dick." Ronin let himself fall in his favorite chair. "What'd you expect? The dude's a pirate. He can't be trusted."

Iris squeezed my hand. "I'm so sorry, Tessa. I was hoping your father could help."

I squeezed back and let go. "He is. He's going to see if he can get me out of the contract with Jack. Meanwhile, I have to come up with my own plan."

Ronin leaned back and crossed his arms behind his head. "What's the plan?"

I smiled. "Well, if you've been paying attention, you know I make things up as I go."

The half-vampire laughed, and a crooked grin worked at his lips. "The best plans are always the half-ass ones."

My back ached and my hip was sore from falling. Add some throbbing in my knees and ankles, and I knew I couldn't stand for much longer. Not if I didn't want to fall face-first on the floor in front of my friends.

I took a step toward my bed and teetered dangerously to the left, only to be steadied by Iris's sturdy hands.

"Here. Let me help," she said, her black hair falling across her concerned face.

With Iris's help, we made it to the end of my bed and I lowered myself with great effort. "I'm fine, thanks," I told her as she let me go.

Who was I kidding? I wasn't fine. My body felt like I'd taken it for a spin in a washing machine.

But something was off. I looked down. "My feet aren't touching the floor anymore? How does that happen?"

Iris pressed her hands on her hips, inspecting me. "What's wrong? There's something else you haven't told us."

Damn, she was perceptive, like a smaller version of Dolores. I raised my eyes to the Dark witch. "I don't think I can use the ley lines anymore. Well, not for very long, anyway. I could barely control them." I took a deep breath and added, "I'm not strong enough. The ley line's energy is much too powerful for this body. I'm too old," I cackled, sounding strangely like Gran. "I wouldn't have made it back if it weren't for my father."

The thought of not being able to use the ley lines did sting a little. It was by far my favorite magical system. The fact that not many witches could control and wield them, or even bend them, made them so much more special to me. Like we were a unique team, an exceptional magical instrument. I'd been really proud of that.

I moved my gaze from Iris to Ronin and forced a smile over my face, trying to hide my disappointment and the loss I felt. "You know what I need?"

Ronin dipped his head my way. "A walker?"

Iris scowled and beat the air with her fist like she was trying to hit him. "You're such an ass."

I laughed. "He's right, though." I chuckled again. "I do. Seriously."

We all laughed at that, me loudest of all until tears streamed down my face. Thank the cauldron I was sitting down because if I was standing, I would have probably peed myself—again.

It felt good to laugh, surrounded by my closest friends. It was like a release of pent-up tension and misery mixed with hope that perhaps things could get better in the future.

Iris walked over to the window and leaned her back against the frame. "What about Ruth? You said she was working on some sort of elixir of youth? How's that going?"

I lost some of my smile. "Her first batch didn't work. She's working on another one. I'm not sure it'll work, though."

"It'll work," argued Iris, tucking a strand of silky black hair behind her ear. "She'll come up with something. Ruth is like the Einstein of potion making. She'll figure something out. I know she will." Her face suddenly took on a pensive cast. "There is another option…"

Her hint of risk piqued my interest. "Why do I get the impression you don't want to tell me?"

Iris clasped her hands before her. "We could ask another demon."

I sat up straighter, shocked I hadn't thought of it myself. "You're right. You're absolutely right." Iris was a genius!

"No, you're both wrong," said Ronin, practically shouting. He leaped to his feet, his eyes dark with warning. "Have you lost your minds? I can't believe I'm hearing this."

"She's right," I agreed, feeling a tiny spark of hope igniting in my gut. "We can ask another demon. My father couldn't because he'd already given me all he could… but another demon? Another demon will want to do this."

"Okay," said Iris, confidence flowing from her. "But you do realize that the demon will request a part of your soul. Are you okay with that?"

I snorted. "He, she, can have any part they want from this body."

"Have you both gone completely mad?" Ronin was staring at us like he wanted to slap the joy off of our faces.

I shook my head. "No. It's brilliant. I just wish I had thought of it." I rocked my body back and forth, swinging my legs to try and get enough forward momentum to get off my bed. It wasn't working.

"You're my sister now," said Iris, and I felt a blush rise to my face. "And I'll do anything for my sister. That's what family's for."

My eighty-year-old heart swelled. "I've always wanted a sister."

"Great." Ronin threw up his hands in a tantrum. "Why don't you both hug and sing kumbaya while you're at it. Then we can all go play in your crazy ass fairy land."

"You're such a mood killer, vampire." I glanced over to Iris. "We can set up the summoning circle here. Do you have a demon in mind?"

"Muranda," answered Iris. "She'll agree to this. But you'll have to... offer her a part of your soul."

Ronin whirled on me, his face screwed up in anger. I didn't like that. If I could have gotten up, I would have punched him, or if my little legs could reach, I would have kicked him in the nads.

"You're going to make a deal with another demon to do what?" he hissed. "Make you young again? And then what? You still have about two weeks left with Captain Jack. Are you going to make another deal with this new demon to break the contract with the soul collector demon? How does that work?"

He did have a point. "Right." I thought about it. "That's two deals with the one demon." My gaze went to Iris. "Is that even a possibility?"

"Everything is possible with demons," answered the Dark witch. She shrugged and said, "It's just a matter of how much you're willing to give."

Damn. It was like going backward, not forward. And I found myself in the exact same position. If I made a deal with a new demon, wouldn't my soul be theirs? Whatever deal I made, my soul would belong to this new demon.

"Oh, look." Iris stared out my bedroom window. "Marcus is here."

Marcus!

"What! What time is it?" I shouted, starting to panic.

I thought I was fine. Guess I'd been lying to myself. My heart pounded and I could barely breathe, to the point where I thought I was having a heart attack.

Ronin checked his phone. "It's half-past five."

"Oh no, oh no! I totally forgot!" I took a breath and said, "Hide!"

"What?" Ronin laughed. "This reminds me of the time Cathy shoved me in the closet because her husband came home early."

Panic crawled up my spine as I threw myself forward, dangerously close to pitching onto the carpet. I tried to reach the floor with my feet, but I couldn't reach it.

Finally, I gave up. "Help," I cried. "I can't get up, and don't you dare say anything, or I'll fry your vampire ass," I warned Ronin, his mouth half-open with whatever he was about to say.

Iris rushed to my aid and gently pulled me to my feet, my knees and ankles popping. "I should have canceled. Why didn't I cancel?"

"Because you had a lot going on," said Ronin.

"Damn. He thinks he's coming to pick me up for our special date tonight." I held my head with my hands. The image of his reaction to seeing me like this made me ill. "What do I do?" I heard the front door open and close and then the sound of muffled voices coming from downstairs.

I took a gasping breath, hunching forward. My muscles wouldn't hold me up. At least not for long. "I need a nap," I said exasperated, feeling today's ley line journey taking a major toll on my body.

"You need a wheelchair," offered Ronin.

Iris glared at him and then turned to me. "I've got a glamour spell kit," she said, speaking quickly. "I can make you look like Catherine Zeta-Jones's sister or Angelina Jolie's?"

I shook my head, not liking how Marcus seeing this version of me was making me feel.

I had to stop acting like this. I was a grown-ass

woman with some serious lady balls. I couldn't hide. I wouldn't hide.

I knew Marcus would be worried but angry most of all. He'd warned me about being impulsive. Taking on a deal with a demon had been reckless, and now I was paying for it.

I quelled my minor panic attack and took charge. "Okay. I can do this," I told myself. I straightened, which was more me stretching my neck, and said, "Let the show begin."

A moment later, a knock came from my bedroom door.

Too late to turn back now.

I swallowed. "Come in."

The bedroom door swung open.

"Are you ready for your special—" Marcus's clean-shaven, handsome face turned to a shocked surprise. His striking gray eyes went hard amid an even harder face.

Oh, dear.

For a long moment, he said nothing, his eyes slowly dilating as he stood in my room with his hand still on the door's handle. I saw his nostrils flare like he was soaking in my scent. The slight widening of his eyes told me he knew this old lady was me. I held my breath, not knowing what might happen or what to say. If he was too mad to talk to me, I could wait.

Our eyes met, and I soaked in those beautiful

gray eyes. Terror constricted my chest as his expression went cold and distant. He might walk away from me this very night. The thought sent a sudden wash of cold shocking through me. If he did, I'd just have to live with it.

Life had thrown me its share of lemons and hard times. I was built for it.

The more he eyed me like a stranger, the more uncomfortable I felt.

Sensing the gigantic awkward moment, Ronin took a step forward. "Can I say something?"

"No," growled Iris and me together.

The half-vampire shrugged, shoved his hands in his jeans pockets, and muttered, "Women."

Marcus seemed to have finally found his voice. "Tessa?" he questioned like he was testing the sound of my name on his lips. He seemed like he couldn't believe he was actually saying it.

"In the flesh," I answered, only realizing after how morbid that sounded. I felt small and awkward. My face flamed, but I couldn't help it.

"We should go." Iris pulled Ronin by the hand and steered him out of the bedroom. "Call me," she said, and then they both disappeared down the stairs.

My gaze fell on Marcus again. His features were pinched, making him look older.

"Are you just going to stand here and not say

anything?" I asked. His intense stare was unsettling, making me feel uncomfortable.

So, what does a witch do in an awkward moment? She finds some way to laugh at herself.

"They say things get better with age. What do you think?" I pulled up my sweater, revealing my shapewear, which didn't do much to hide the fact that I was an eighty-year-old woman wearing some Spanx.

I looked over to Marcus, and my laughter died in my throat.

"What? Too soon?" I asked, pulling down my sweater. *Okay, bad idea.*

The chief blinked a few times, his eyes narrowing. I could hear the low and angry undertones to his next words. "Tessa. What the hell did you do?"

14

Okay. Not *exactly* the reaction I was expecting. But it could have been worse.

"That much of a shock, huh?" I sighed, a smile tugging at my lips. "I have to say that I'm over it myself. It was hard at first. I won't lie, but I've come to terms with the fact that I've aged fifty years in one day. Best birthday ever."

Marcus clenched his jaw, seemingly to finally get over the initial shock. "What is this, Tessa? Please tell me it's some glamour spell."

I could tell by his voice that he didn't believe it was. It probably didn't smell like a glamour, which was kind of gross thinking he'd smelled me.

"It's not," I answered, taking him in. He wore a fitted soft gray sweater under his usual black winter coat, tucked in his fitted jeans splayed snugly against his thick, powerful thighs. He looked amazing.

I felt a tug in my chest as I thought about our date tonight and the "after-party" later. I seriously doubted he'd want to go through with it, after his cold and hostile reaction at seeing some Spanx on an eighty-year-old body. What would happen if he saw me naked? Yeah, not going to happen.

"This is because of the deal you made with the soul collector?" His brows were pinched when he met my eyes. "I knew this would happen. I knew it. You can't make deals with demons and think they won't try to take more than what was offered. A demon, Tessa. How could you be so careless? Look what happened to you."

Now I was pissed. "My father's a demon." I struggled to rein in my feelings. "And I have to say... that so far... he's a pretty decent guy. I like him. Demon or not. He's been good to me."

Marcus's expression shifted. It was only for a moment, but in that second I saw furious rage and violent savagery on his face. He regained his cool composure quickly, but traces of those hidden emotions thickened his voice.

"And that makes what happened to you okay?" he growled.

"No. Of course not," I said, my voice shaking with a tide of emotions. "But I don't think you can label demons as all bad. Just like us, I think there are the right sort and the wrong sort. I just happened to have made a deal with the wrong sort."

Marcus dragged his hands over his face and started to pace my room, some of that primal rage leaving him. "What about Ruth?" he asked hopefully as he spun to face me. "I've never known a better witch at potions. Can she help?"

I shook my head, feeling a burn in my ankles. "So far, what she's given me hasn't worked. She's still working on something." I eyed the chair facing my bed, the one Ronin liked to sit in, and gauged the distance, wondering if I could make it without falling on my face.

"When did this happen?" he asked softly. "When did you... change?"

"I woke up this afternoon looking like this."

"But you were fine yesterday? You were still... you?" His voice was raw with emotions, sounding like he was trying to speak through a sore throat.

"I was," I answered, my eyes still on the chair. "I've been feeling some aches and pains but nothing like this. Nothing remotely close to this."

Disbelief shone in his gray eyes. "That demon is sucking the life out of you," he said irately. "And for what? To save a few souls from mortals who were already dead? Who had lived a long life?"

"One of those souls you're talking about

happened to be my gran's. There was no way around it." I sighed. "I'm not having this conversation with you again. What's done is done. There's no going back. I took the deal. It's over."

"You should have never taken that deal in the first place."

I sighed with impatience. "Marcus, please..."

"All of this is because of it."

"I don't need you to rub it in my face. I know what I did."

Marcus took a slow breath. "Can your father help you?" he asked, not listening to me at all. "You told me he saved your life. He can do it again."

"No," I answered, noticing how he kept his distance from me, which stung a little. He hadn't touched me either. It wasn't like I hadn't noticed. "He's already saved me once. He's all out of 'saving Tessa's life.' There's nothing he can do for me."

Emotions flashed over his features too fast to be understood. "You're going to die," he said, exasperated. "This is going to kill you."

"That's old news. Get with the program."

Marcus's mouth snapped shut. "This isn't funny. How can you think this is funny?" He was practically shouting.

If I didn't know he was worried about me, I would have had House throw him out on his ass. Even now he was pushing it.

I ground my teeth. "No, it's not funny, but I'm not about to wallow in self-pity either."

The chief was silent in thought. With deep concern in his gaze, he looked at me and said, "Damnit, Tessa. How could you let this happen?"

"I didn't *let* anything happen."

"You know what I mean," he said. "If you hadn't taken that deal, you wouldn't be standing here, looking like your entire life passed you by."

Okay, I'd had enough. "Can you just shut up and help me to the chair before I fall and break a hip."

Marcus looked startled at my request. After a few beats, he was next to me, holding me up in his strong, muscular arms. One hand gripped my elbow ever so gently for such rough hands while the other was warm against my waist. I turned to face him, his hands tracing a delicious path around my waist. His hard body pressed tightly against my back, and it took a great amount of self-control to not let myself fall against him.

My pulse was pounding, and I was suddenly aware of how much I was sweating. Well, that wasn't good.

He was warm and solid, and I let him lead, using him to keep my balance as my feet slid against the hardwood floors.

"Thank you," I croaked, inches from his ear, and then cleared my throat, embarrassed.

His breath was hot and moved my hair as he guided me to the chair, like I was the most precious thing in the world, as though getting me to that chair was his sole purpose in life.

But at the rate we were going, I'd get to the chair around tomorrow morning.

"I'm not made of glass," I guffawed. "You can move faster. I won't break."

"I'm sorry," he said, his voice low and clipped, and his grip on me grew tighter. There wasn't much room between us, and I liked it. Part of me never wanted him to move away. "I'm sorry about how I spoke to you. I shouldn't have said those things."

I pulled my eyes away before he saw the tears that threatened to break there. "You were in shock and upset. It's fine. You were expecting hot, thirty-year-old Tessa. Not Granny Tess."

The chief was silent. "You make a hot grandmother."

A thread of heat coiled in my center, and I cackled a laugh. "And I like inappropriately younger men apparently. What's that called again? Not a cougar... oh, right. I'm a sabertooth."

Marcus laughed, the sound sending deep, lovely vibrations through my back. "Is that really a thing?"

I missed the sound of that laugh. "Oh, yeah. I read it online somewhere," I told him, concentrating on putting one foot in front of the other. "Sixty-plus women who date younger guys."

The chief made a sound in his throat. "So, what does that make me?"

I grinned. "My gigolo."

We both laughed, finally making it to the chair. I sat, happy to give my poor ankles and knees a well-deserved rest but sad about the sudden loss of Marcus's body heat.

He moved and sat at the edge of my bed so we were facing each other. I felt another rush of heat flare from my middle to my face at the intensity of his eyes.

"What can I get you?" he asked.

I smiled. "A gallon of wine?"

The chief smiled and glanced at the floor, his eyes dramatically sad. They tugged on my heart. He opened his mouth and then shut it. I could see he was struggling with whatever words he wanted to say.

He pulled his gaze back to me. "How…"

"How long do I have?" I guessed from the sadness rippling on his face. "A week maybe? Probably less?" But at the rate I'd aged, I was guessing I had a few days tops. Then I was going to join Gran wherever dead witches went after they died. Maybe there was a place just for us witches? Maybe I was just fooling myself.

When I looked back at Marcus, grief, and pain reflected in those mesmerizing gray eyes. "Tessa..."

"Don't." I stiffened and then swallowed, my throat tight. "Don't do that."

"Do what?"

"Don't pity me. Just don't." Because I was about to lose control. I couldn't let myself. I needed to put an iron clamp on my emotions. I needed to be strong.

He watched me a moment, a hint of a smile on that glorious mouth of his. "It's a lot to take in. I wasn't... expecting that."

I snorted. "You're telling me!" I smiled, wishing I could tackle him on my bed but knowing it would take a crane to get me out of this chair.

Seeing some of the tension lessen around Marcus's shoulders, I felt myself relax.

"Don't worry about me," I told him, my chest constricting with a sudden pain that had nothing to do with my elderly body. "I'll be fine." Probably not, but what else was I supposed to say?

Marcus clenched his jaw. "What time does the soul collector show up?"

"Around ten p.m."

Marcus looked at his watch and then back at me. "He'll be here in a few hours." The chief watched me as he tossed the hair from his eyes. "I know you. I know you've thought of something. Do I dare ask what that is?"

I looked across my bedroom to my window.

A smile curled my lips. "I have a plan."

15

What was this master plan, you ask? Well, it wasn't much. Try coming up with a master plan when every single bone and joint in your body is screaming in searing pain to the point there isn't enough Tylenol in the world to alleviate it.

The said plan was to stay in my room and wait it out.

It was the best I could come up with. If I didn't show, hopefully, Jack would get the message and leave. We'd never discussed a vacation or time off. Was I even allowed time off? Who cared? This was me taking it.

I didn't know what the repercussions from my insubordination would be, but I knew there would be some. It couldn't be worse than aging fifty years overnight. But then again, maybe it could.

I sat in my chair facing the window, a vial of purple liquid in my right hand and my cell phone in the other as I stared out to the front of the house where the soul collector came to collect me every single night at ten sharp for the past weeks.

I glanced down at my cell phone. "It's ten past. He's not here."

"Has he ever been late?" asked Ronin, sitting on the edge of the bed where Marcus had been sitting a while ago.

I'd sent Marcus home. I was tired of him staring at me like I might suddenly keel over and die. The overwhelming sadness and helplessness had thrown me over the edge. Watching him watching me like that was too much. Not only was it increasingly uncomfortable, but it was also irritating. He would have to get used to me not being around him if my age continued to progress.

"No. He's always been on time," I answered, edging forward in my chair and looking out the window again.

"Guess whatever your father planned on doing worked," offered Iris, standing with her arms crossed next to me. "Maybe this is finally over. Maybe you're free."

I shook my head. "It's not over. It can't be that simple, but it's changed. The fact that he's not here yet means something."

I'd signed a contract with the soul collector, and the only way to get out of that contract was if I died or if I or someone else offered something better to the demon. I didn't think another idiot in the world would offer his or her services to him. The said idiot—me.

Iris turned her dark eyes on me. The light in the room cast a shadow on her pretty face. "My offer still stands. If you want to summon Muranda, we can still do it."

Ronin growled. "Not this again."

I gave Iris a quick smile. "I know. Let me think about it." But the more I did, the more it sounded insane. I was in enough trouble dealing with one demon. Adding another one made my insides squirm.

"Think about it like this," continued Iris. "If your father managed to close the deal with the soul collector, all we have to concentrate on is giving you your youth back."

That perked my attention. If Iris was right, and if my father had managed to square a deal with Jack, maybe, just maybe, making a deal with another demon to restore my youth wasn't that bad.

The bed creaked as Ronin leaned forward and rested his elbows on his thighs, the tension clear on his shoulders. "Are you planning on doing this every night until the end of your contract?"

"If it works, yeah."

"Are you going to drink that?" Iris's face was stern, reminding me of Dolores.

"Yeah. Why didn't you drink Ruth's potion?" asked Ronin.

I lifted the vial in my hand. The liquid was a dark purple in the dim light of the room. "I didn't want to see the disappointment on her face if it didn't work. She worked for hours on this."

Ronin raised his head. "Well, she's not here now. Try it."

"Okay. Here goes. Bottoms up." Exhaling, I pulled out the cork stopper, tilted the vial to my mouth, and downed it.

The liquid was warm and, surprisingly, I felt a wash of energy pour out and swirl up to settle around my belly. My entire body grew loose as a warmth flowed into me, carrying a soothing ripple of shivers with it. A sudden swirl of magic pulsed evenly through me. It hung within me for a moment and then nothing. The throbbing pains in my bones soothed until I couldn't feel them anymore. In fact, I felt rejuvenated. I felt amazing. Better than I had all day.

My heart leaped. Could this have worked? Could Ruth's elixir of youth have reversed the premature aging?

But one look at the hand that still held the vial,

and my hope evaporated. "It didn't work," I announced, my voice tight with anger.

Iris put a hand on my shoulder. "I'm sorry, Tessa. But we'll find a way to fix this. I know we can."

I looked out the window again, trying hard not to let my emotions overrun me. I needed my head screwed on right to figure this out. And I would.

Still, there was no sign of the soul collector. That lifted my mood a little.

The sound of feet climbing up the steps along with voices pulled my attention beyond my opened bedroom door.

Dolores, Beverly, and Ruth all clambered onto the platform at the end of the stairs.

Dolores stopped at the threshold and leaned heavily against it. "Why couldn't you pick a room that wasn't in the attic," she panted. "I think I just lost a lung climbing all those stairs."

I gave her a tight smile, knowing she could have asked House to help her, but I also knew that would show signs of aging and weakness. These sisters would have none of it.

Beverly brushed past her, swinging her hips. "I don't know what you're talking about." She grabbed her rear end with both hands and said, "Climbing stairs is great to keep your butt looking like an apple. Like mine," she added happily, her red kitten heels clacking on the wood floor. Climbing up stairs in any heels was impressive.

Dolores grunted, finally letting go of the wall. "If you mean the Big Apple, then yes, the size's about right."

Ruth walked in last. "Tessa, did it work?" Her smiling, cheery face fell at the sight of me. Shoulders slumped, she added, "Oh. It didn't work. I thought I had it this time. I even added gremlin poop. It's really potent in magical qualities and rejuvenating properties."

I did not have to know that. But worse than knowing, I'd just swallowed some.

Ronin snorted, and I shot him a look that made him squirm where he was.

Ruth just stood there looking so sad, as though I'd just accidentally run over her puppy with the Volvo, that I managed to get up on my own and shuffle toward her.

"See?" I said, crossing my bedroom. My bones cracked and popped but it was hardly noticeable. "I wouldn't have been able to do this without your potion. So, it did work, somewhat. It took away some of the pain and stiffness."

Ruth's face lit up a little, but she couldn't hide the wetness in her eyes. "Here," she said and handed me a wooden cane that I hadn't even noticed she had brought with her.

I took the cane in my hand, surprised at finding it warm to the touch with a slight pulsing. I stared at it a moment, my eyes traveling over the multitude of birds and vines.

I looked up at Ruth because though she was the shortest of my aunts, she was now taller than me. "This is Gran's cane. I thought it was lost." My thoughts went back to that night when the soul collector had taken Gran's soul and had killed me in the process.

Dolores put a hand on her hip, her expression somber. "We took it with us back home that night... well... you know which one I'm talking about."

"The one when I died?"

Dolores snapped her fingers at me. "That would be the one."

Ruth brushed a strand of white hair from her face that had come apart from her bun. "I thought you could use it, if my... well, I'm sure Mum would have wanted you to have it. She loved you very much."

"I loved her too." My eyes burned at those words. "Thank you." I brought the cane down and tested it, leaning my weight on it and finding it comfortable, like having another leg. "This is great. Now I can maneuver without dreading falling on my face."

"If you had on some old linen robes, you could

pass for her twin," said Ronin with a stupid smile on his face.

"He's right," said Iris, moving to sit next to Ronin on the bed. "You really do look like her."

I raised a brow. "Well, she was my gran."

"What's this?" Beverly had picked up my pant suit Jack had given me. She brought it to her face and grimaced. "Smells like the inside of Lorenzo Russo's car. Tessa? When's the last time you had this dry cleaned?"

"The soul collector gave it to me," I told her, seeing the other aunts' attention on me. "I don't think it's meant to be dry cleaned."

Beverly's face pulled into a tight, sour expression. She dropped the suit over the chair, looking like it had fleas crawling over it. She checked her hands and then wiped them on her jeans. "Speaking of that dreadful demon, where is he? He should have been here by now."

"Demons can't enter Davenport House," stated Dolores, which only confirmed my suspicions. "The multitude of wards and spells make it impossible. Add the ley line protection, and you have yourself a bunker against all things demon. They can't penetrate it."

Beverly fanned herself dramatically. "Speaking of *penetrating* things. I've got a date tomorrow with Shane O'Connor. He's recently divorced and gorgeous. He's got Paul Newman's eyes and face, and he happens to like voluptuous women."

"You mean he likes your Big Apple butt?" laughed Dolores, her long face pulled in a smile.

Beverly scowled at her sister. "You're just jealous because you haven't been laid since the turn of the century."

Dolores's eyes disappeared under her thick scowl. "You throw your vagina around like it's a sale at Macy's."

Beverly placed her hands on her hips, glaring at her sister. "Vaginas weren't meant for just the birth canal. They were meant to be used and explored, to enjoy them. We can't let the men have all the fun."

Yeah, this was not a conversation I wanted to hear. "Uh... can we talk about something other than your vajayjays?"

"Shh. Tess." Ronin waved a hand at me, his attention on my aunts. "I want to hear this," he added, winning a smack behind his head from Iris.

My gaze flicked between my aunts, not liking the animosity that was growing. "Guys. Don't fight—"

I bent over. My breath came in a ragged gasp. I twisted as agony vibrated through me, and every nerve ending throbbed into a burn. The pain went all the way from my skull to my toes. It felt like... like my body was being pulled in every direction at once.

Oh. Shit.

"Oh, no," I said, panic unfurling in my body. "Something's happening." Not letting go of the cane, I wrapped my arms around my middle. "Something's wrong."

Ruth was the first one next to me since, well, she had been standing right there. She gripped my elbow. "I feared this might happen."

Gritting my teeth, I asked, "What are you talking about?"

"This might be a side effect of the elixir of youth." She looked at me with a slightly embarrassed expression and added with a whisper, "Cramps and some intestinal failure."

Fantastic. But this wasn't it. "I don't think this is what's happening to me. This is—"

I felt myself pulled forward. The last thing I saw was Ruth's round eyes as darkness fell.

16

Somewhere, sirens began to wail.

The darkness lifted away to reveal light and motion with the sound of distant traffic. Dizzy and cold, I became acutely aware that I was outside without a winter coat.

With Gran's cane still grasped in my grip, I used it to balance myself as I took a better look at my surroundings.

Streetlights cast down pools of light onto the shadowed sidewalk and dark street. Rows of neatly tight houses flanked both sides of a road that disappeared beyond a hill nested between tall trees and neatly trimmed shrubbery.

There was no snow, but the wind was still icy. In mid-January in Maine, there's still lots of snow. I had no idea where I was, but I was definitely not home.

The sound of feet approaching brought my heart into my mouth. I spun around, which was more of a teetering shuffle, and pointed Gran's cane at a tall, thin man wearing a dark suit.

The soul collector's face rippled in a mix of frustration and disappointment. "I had hoped the aging wouldn't happen so fast with you. With your family history and all."

Anger twisted my gut. "You sonovabitch. You knew this would happen?" I seethed, the cane still pointed at his chest, wishing I had the energy to whack him over the head with it.

With an annoyed expression, Jack moved the cane from his chest with a finger, his white eyes alight under the shadow of his hat. "The suit was supposed to protect you from this very thing. It was weaved from the silk of demon worms and the blood of the demon Zazzle. He's quite good at cards, you know. I think it has something to do with his two sets of arms."

"I despise you."

He pressed his lips together and said, "I've been perfecting it for over a century. The best of its class. How utterly disappointing to find that it didn't work on you. I can understand why my other mortal assistants aged. But you? You were supposed to be the exception. With your demon father, you were supposed to be the one. I had high hopes for you.

Imagine my surprise to find out that you're nothing but a dud."

I wasn't sure what made me angrier. The fact that he'd done this to other mortals, or that I was supposed to be "the one."

I jabbed the cane into his chest, hard. Not smart, poking a Greater demon like that, but he was pissing me off. "Me aging wasn't part of the deal. I didn't sign up for this."

Again, Jack moved the cane from his chest with a finger. "Would you have refused to save your grandmother's soul otherwise?" His tone was bitter. "Would you have let her go if I told you that you might age prematurely while being in my service?"

"Age prematurely? I'm a freaking fossil about to expire. Yeah. That wasn't part of the deal."

Jack just watched me a moment, his hairless brow high. "Curious that it seemed to have progressed immensely in one night." He drew back, his expression both disgusted and amazed, and I shook with the rising of my anger. "Why aren't you wearing the suit I made for you?"

My mouth dropped open. "Are you serious? Even if I wanted to, it probably doesn't even fit me anymore. I've shrunk."

"I noticed."

"And I'm wider than I was for some strange reason." Which was odd, but there you have it.

My knees began to ache again, and I realized Ruth's tonic was about to expire. So much for that. Now I wished I had a bit more. Hell, I should be carrying it around with me like a portable IV.

"How did you bring me here?" I asked, leaning on Gran's cane for support.

Jack stared at me like I was a simpleton. "I'm a demon. I'm blessed with vast demon magic. Teleportation is very standard. Any low-class demon can teleport."

I shook my head. "No. I mean. How were you able to get me out of Davenport House? You shouldn't have been able to." Or so I thought. Maybe my aunts had been wrong about the house.

Jack's eyes flicked to mine. "The contract you signed binds you to me. I know where you are at all times. And no amount of witch magic and wards can keep you away from me. I own you, whether you like it or not."

"That sounds a little kinky," I said, and I almost laughed at the shocked expression on the demon's face. "Could you have at least thought about bringing me a coat or something? It's freezing. It's winter. I'm old, tired, and cold."

"Yes. That will be a problem." Jack snapped his fingers, and a heavy woolen cloak was wrapped around my shoulders, giving me instant warmth.

I could have thanked him, but it was his fault I was here.

"Come along now, Tessa." Jack's attention flicked to something behind me. "We can't afford to get tangled with the human authorities."

I followed his gaze and whirled around.

Crushed against the trunk of a tree was a white sedan, the taillights flashing red. Yellow light spilled from the front of the car, and through them, I could see smoke rising from beneath the bent hood. Now I understood the sounds of the sirens.

"Why are we at the scene of an accident?"

Jack gestured at me with his briefcase and said, "Because you're working."

"Working?" Dreading what I was about to find, I followed the demon to the side of the car, the sudden burst of adrenaline welcomed, as it helped propel my stiff legs faster.

Using the cane for balance, I leaned over and looked inside the car. "There's no one inside," I said as I pulled myself up. If there was no one inside the car... then...

Jack had moved to a spot about ten feet from the car and was looking down.

Heart in my throat, I managed to shuffle my way next to him. The blood left my face.

A young woman, around my age, lay on the asphalt, her body bent and broken, limbs twisted in ways that shouldn't be possible. She was on her side. Blood trickled from her open mouth, and then her blue eyes met mine.

"Shit. She's alive! Quick, call 911," I said out loud and then realized I didn't have my phone with me.

"The call's been made." Jack knelt next to the woman. "Tessa. Meet Gloria. Hello, Gloria," said the demon, like he was having a casual conversation at a party. "Were you speeding again? You couldn't stop at just one gin and tonic. Could you? Mmm. You know what they say? Don't drink and drive."

Ah, hell. "We have to help her. She's still alive."

Jack cocked his head to the side. "Severe internal bleeding. Punctured lung. Her heart is just about to give out. She's also got a brain bleed. There's nothing the paramedics can do. She'll be dead before they get here." Jack pulled out his pocket watch. "Gloria," he said looking at her with a smile that made me sick to my stomach. "You're going to die in precisely thirty seconds."

The woman's eyes widened in fear. Her lips moved, trying to formulate words, but only blood sputtered out.

I didn't think I could hate the soul collector more than at this very moment.

"I hate you," I said and then looked to the distant, glowing city. I looked out over the city, seeing an ambulance racing down the highway with its bulbs flashing and sirens wailing.

"Get in line," snapped the demon, not missing the innuendo in his words. Clearly, he had enemies.

At my silence, he added with a smile like he was about to relay some deep secret, "The inebriated, the alcoholics, the party animals are the easiest souls to collect. See, even if she agrees that we save her life tonight, I predict in a month or two, she'll be dead. And we'll have a soul to collect."

I frowned. I wouldn't be collecting souls in a month. Maybe he meant we as in he would have another assistant.

Jack adjusted his hat. "Do your job. Have her agree to the contract or I will expire you." From inside his jacket, the demon pulled out a contract and handed it to me.

"What makes you so sure she'll agree?"

"Because you have a trustworthy face. You look like everyone's grandmother. Who doesn't trust a grandma?"

I felt like throwing up. He was going to use my new look to his advantage.

Stifling my anger, I took the contract from him in my trembling hand and bent over the dying woman.

"Gloria," I said. "I'm sorry this has happened to you. And like my... partner suggested, you are going to die. And I know that you know it's true." I stared at her frightened blue eyes filled with pain. Her attention flicked to Jack. I saw the horror and then the slow recognition of what he was. Next was the acceptance, or maybe she was telling herself she was hallucinating, which was a lot easier to accept. "But we can save you. All you have to do is agree to offer your soul to the soul collector, and you will live." Her eyes flicked back to me. "You won't feel any more pain," I added, hating every single word coming out of my mouth. "You'll be exactly how you were, right before the accident. Do you agree? Do you offer your soul in exchange for your life?"

Gloria's mouth moved but again, no words came out. But she didn't have to say anything. I could see it in her eyes, and the slight nod of her head. Yes.

"Good enough," said Jack, his eyes greedily on her, having seen the same thing as I did. "Get her signature."

I glared at him over my shoulder. "She can't sign a contract in her state."

Jack rolled his eyes, which was a very mundane thing to do. "A fingerprint with her blood will do." He let out a long breath. "Haven't you learned anything?"

I flipped him off, probably not the smartest thing to do, but right now I wasn't scared of the demon anymore. What's the worst he could do to me now? He'd already made me into a fossil.

When I was sure he wasn't going to fry me on the spot, I turned back to Gloria. Bracing myself, and using the cane as support, I lowered to the ground on my knees next to the dying woman. My knees made the sound of popcorn in the microwave. My joints screamed in protest. I was not getting back up anytime soon.

"Gloria," I said, "I need to take your hand now. I'm going to press one of your fingers to the contract. Okay?"

When she nodded, I grabbed her right hand, which thank the cauldron had blood on it and gently pressed her index finger on the signature line leaving a bloody fingerprint.

"Thank you." I was going to hell for this.

"Shake her hand. Go on now." Jack beamed, looking pleased with himself.

I stared at Gloria's hand, which I still held in my own. Part of me wanted to tell the demon to fuck off and try to heal her, but it was too late. The contract was signed.

"Tessa," growled Jack. "I'm running out of time." I couldn't help but notice that he'd said that *he* was running out of time, and not that she was. Strange.

Cursing, I placed my hand in hers, her skin cold and clammy, and there was barely a pulse on her wrist. I gripped her hand tightly, knowing how wrong this was and knowing I was about to lose more of my own life force. But seeing her in so much pain, all I wanted was to help her. I couldn't stand it.

And just like every other soul I'd collected, as I gripped her hand firmly in mine, I felt a sudden pulse of energy. Then came a spark of light that sealed the deal. The spark marked Gloria's soul as the soul collector's.

"Thank you for your business." Jack seized the contract from my free hand and slipped it inside his jacket.

With my hand still clamped in hers, I waited. But not for long. I watched as her face went through the same vortex of emotions as all the others—the fear and then the disbelief, acceptance, and finally hope as the pain vanished from her expression.

And then slowly, very slowly, Gloria sat up. She blinked at me. "Is this real? Are you an angel?" She snatched her hand back when she realized I was still holding on to it.

More like the angel of death. "I'm sorry," I told her, feeling a giant wave of regret wash through me. "I'm sorry about all of it." It seemed every time I took a soul, a part of me died. Literally.

"Let's go."

Jack hurled me to my feet, and I smacked his hands from me once I was steady, not wanting him to touch me. I didn't want anything to do with him.

The sirens were loud now. The ambulance was

almost upon us as I shuffled behind Jack until we crossed the street and reached the sidewalk opposite the scene of the accident.

I felt a slight fever, a weakness I hadn't felt before. I knew I'd just lost another few years. I couldn't keep this up for much longer.

"Hurry up," called Jack over his shoulder. "We need to stay hidden from the human authorities. Quickly before they arrive. We have lots of work to do tonight. Many more souls to collect before the night is over."

"I'm going as fast as I can," I growled, cursing him with my eyes. My stomach clenched as I asked, "How many more?"

"Twenty-six are scheduled for tonight," he said without stopping. "We need to collect three hundred before the week is over."

"Three hundred?" I cried. "You're mad."

Jack shrugged. "Who isn't a little mad."

My knees buckled and I halted before they gave way. "I can't keep going like this. I'm not going to make it. I'll never make it to the end of the week."

Jack stopped and turned. "I've thought about that. I'll just make some adjustments to the suit. That way you won't age. It'll keep you preserved for a little while longer."

"A little while longer?"

"I've had the best success rate with you by my

side," said Jack, his voice pointedly cheerful. "A seventy-three percent increase. You're my good luck charm. Must be the way you look. And even better that you've aged. Who doesn't trust Granny?"

"You're a sick bastard," I said dryly.

The thought of what I wanted to say next had my gut in a twisted blend of emotion—anger, doubt, and the fear that I was about to expire from a life that I'd just barely started—a life without my family and friends. Let's not pretend I wasn't thinking about Marcus because I was.

I pressed the cane on the ground and leaned on it. "Once my contract is over, will I change back to what I looked like before? Will I get my youth back? Will I be thirty again?"

He narrowed his eyes at me. "No. The only thing I can do is slow the process."

Not the answer I wanted, but I could still take Iris's advice and seek another demon to offer whatever was left of my soul to get those years back. Hopefully.

"Okay, not so bad," I told myself. "I can manage another thirteen days working for you, though I really do hate you. And then, I'll never have to see you ever again." Now that brought a smile to my face. Hell, I thought I might break into a dance.

Jack peered at me from under his hat. "How's that?"

I raised my brows. "Because my contract will be over. I agreed to one month. And that month is over in thirteen days. Don't even try to screw me over. Not going to happen."

The demon's face was empty of emotion. "Your contract with me does not terminate in thirteen days."

I flinched in my panic. "What? What are you talking about? We made a deal. You can't go back on it." That I knew for a fact.

Jack splayed a hand on his chest and managed to look innocent. "I'm not. I'm honoring our deal."

"Which was one month's service."

A slow smile began to spread over the demon's face, and my heart pounded. "I'm afraid not. You signed a *lifetime's* service. Not a month's."

I tried to take a deep breath, but I felt like there wasn't enough air. The sirens were blaring now. They must be right next to Gloria, but I couldn't look away from the demon.

"You're lying," I croaked, my voice sounding old, withered, and tired.

Jack reached inside his jacket and handed me a contract. "This is your contract. Didn't you read it before you signed?"

My stomach twisted and everything started to spin. I remember that night well. And I remember signing. I never read the damn contract.

I held the contract up to the light. Yeah. That was my signature. I'd signed a contract with a demon, but I'd never read it. You'd think I'd be smarter when I turned thirty.

Guess not.

Jack pointed to a small paragraph just above my signature. "The devil's in the detail," he guffawed.

I glanced down and read: *I, Tessa Davenport, hereby offer my services to the soul collector number SC889-N55 in perpetuity.*

"You see, Tessa. I'm not about to get rid of my lucky charm." Satisfaction in his every motion, Jack grabbed the contract back and slipped it inside his jacket. "You are mine until your very last breath."

Well, this wasn't part of my plan.

17

Who signs a contract with a demon and does not look at the fine print?

Yours truly, apparently.

I'd barely slept a wink after my night out with the soul collector. I'd been numb for the four hours following this new information. I mean, who wouldn't? I'd signed my life away to a demon without even knowing it. I was a fool. The biggest fool that ever existed. The biggest fool in the damn universe.

I was a witch—a Davenport witch. And Davenport witches *always* read a contract's fine print. I should have known better.

The demon had tricked me. He'd used my emotions, used my scared out of my mind about losing my grandmother's soul as a distraction. He took a chance that I wouldn't read the contract in my rush to save my gran. And he'd been rewarded. The bastard had conned me.

Anger welled until it made my blood boil and my head spin. Thinking of boiling, I imagined shoving Jack in one of Ruth's tub-size steaming cauldrons until all that was left were his floating bones and his stupid hat. It was a great visual.

"Tess? You okay? Here... let me get the door for you."

Ronin brushed past me and opened the back passenger door to his black BMW 7 Series.

He'd never offered to open the door for me before. Ever. Not that he should. But I was angry at everything, me most of all. I hated that he did it now because of what I looked like. I found I couldn't speak without saying something I'd regret. Ronin was the first friend I'd made coming back to Hollow Cove. I wasn't about to lose him.

Clamping my mouth shut, I stuffed the cane in first, and using the door for balance, I managed to get myself through the opening and onto the seat.

The sound of leather pulled as Iris spun around in her front seat. "You look like you want to peel the skin off of someone," she said, just as Ronin shut my door.

I unclenched my jaw. "That's because I do."

Iris's eyes were wide with sadness. "We're going

to figure this out. You hear me? But first, we're taking you out for your birthday. You need a little cheering up."

I watched as Ronin got behind the wheel of his car, shut the door, and turned the ignition. "That was yesterday." Worst birthday ever. Probably my last.

"And you didn't celebrate it," she continued, as Ronin backed out of the driveway and turned onto the street. "Let us do something nice for you. Okay? You needed to get out of the house. Change it up for a while." She hesitated. "I know what it's like to spiral down that darkness. I've been there. You need to pull yourself out."

"I'm not spiraling down anywhere."

She cocked a brow. "You are. I can see it in your eyes."

I moved my tongue over the two holes on my upper gums that weren't there yesterday. If I kept losing teeth at this rate, I'd need dentures by tomorrow. "It's called being pissed. All I can think of are all the ways I can kill Jack. *How to boil a demon.* Didn't I read that in one of your books?"

Ronin snorted as he stopped at a stop sign. "She has a point. The demon did trick her."

Iris sent a glare in Ronin's direction. "That's part of what being a demon is. They are master tricksters. That's nothing new. He saw an opening... and he took it."

"That opening being the rest of my life," I snapped. I took a deep breath, trying to reel in my emotions before I bit the head off of my only friends. "It's all my fault. If I had taken a few seconds and read the damn contract, I wouldn't be in this mess. I'd be old, yeah, but still alive. Still able to look for a cure for my premature ageism."

"Is that even a thing?" Ronin glanced at me through the rearview mirror, a smirk on his face.

I shrugged. "No idea, but the point is, if I had more time, I could figure this out. I know I could, but I'm all out of time."

Iris frowned. "But you said the soul collector would fix that. He was going to work on that suit. Keep you alive. He doesn't want you to die. He needs you to keep working for him. Didn't he call you his lucky charm?"

I looked out the window. "I don't think he can keep me alive for much longer. With or without his suit. Once I'm gone, he'll just find another replacement. I'm just the flavor of the month."

Iris shook her head. "I hate seeing you like this."

"Like what?" I shrugged. "Old?" Though I knew that's not what she meant.

The Dark witch frowned. "No. Of course not. I mean like this... defeated," she said, her voice clipped.

"Don't worry." I looked back at her. "I'm not

defeated. I'm not planning on going down easy. I'm going to find a way to get out of my contract." Or die trying.

"How?" asked Ronin. "Please don't start with that summoning another demon stuff again. That's crazy."

I met his eyes through the rearview mirror and said, "I'm going to kill him."

Silence. They didn't believe me.

"I'm going to kill him," I repeated, my mouth dry. "That's how I'll get out of my contract." I just didn't know how I was planning on doing that at the moment. I might be old and frail and dangerously out of time, but one thing I still had going for me was an imagination. It would take lots of imaginings to figure out a way to end a Greater demon.

Their continued silence only cemented my belief that they didn't think I could do it. And, of course, they felt sorry for me. I hated that. Pity. I didn't need anyone's pity.

"Do we really need to go out to eat?" I asked, wanting to change the subject. "Ruth was very happy to cook something for all of us. I don't want to see anyone. I don't want anyone seeing me and recognizing me."

"Trust me," said Ronin with a smile. "No one will recognize you."

That didn't make me feel any better.

"We're here," announced Iris, turning around and looking out the car window.

We pulled up in front of Ristorante da Vinci, the only Italian restaurant in Hollow Cove. I'd only been here once before with Iris, and the food was amazing.

Okay, my mood suddenly lifted at the prospect of hot, freshly baked bread topped with melting butter.

After Iris helped me out of the car—because let's face it, I couldn't manage on my own—we entered the restaurant and followed a hostess toward a table for four next to the large window that overlooked the street.

"Menus are on the table," said our hostess, a young twenty-something brunette, whose eyes were glued on Ronin. "I'll send your waitress to take your orders in a few minutes."

Not thinking I could squeeze myself into the window seat without making a scene, I grabbed the closest chair and sat with Gran's cane propped against the side of the chair.

"I'm starving," announced Iris in the seat next to me. She grabbed a menu and began flipping through it.

I snatched up the menu in front of me and opened it, blinking at the blurred writing and images. Inconspicuously, I brought the menu closer and then moved it further back. I couldn't make out a single word. It was like someone had spilled water on the ink and then decided to do some finger painting. Oh, goodie. I was losing my eyesight. Excellent.

A moment later, a short, curvy Asian woman bumped her hip against our table. "Are you ready to order?" Smiling at us, she placed two baskets of freshly baked bread on our table. Her eyes lingered on Ronin, though he didn't seem to notice since he was too busy reading the menu.

Iris cleared her throat. "I'm having the veggie pizza."

I reached out and grabbed a bread, practically salivating as I spread nearly an inch of butter over it. I tore off a piece with my gnarled fingers, realizing the sight of them didn't bother me anymore and stuffed it in my mouth. My eyes nearly rolled in the back of my head. It was all I could do not to moan. Freshly baked bread was the best thing in life as far as I was concerned. With butter.

"And you, sir?" she asked Ronin.

"I'll have the vegetarian calzone with a side of fries," said the half-vampire. "And a bottle of Nebbiolo Langhe. Three glasses."

The waitress wrote it all down. "And what will your grandmother have?"

A chunk of bread came flying out of my mouth. *Grandmother?*

Both Ronin and Iris stilled like I'd hexed them

with a solidifying spell. The waitress looked down at me, expectantly.

"I'll have the veggie pizza as well." I was too embarrassed to tell my friends that I couldn't read the menu.

"Great." The waitress picked up our menus and disappeared toward the back of the restaurant.

Yes, it came as a bit of a shock to be called a grandmother when only a few days ago I was in the body of a thirty-year-old. But I had to accept that woman was gone now.

"It's fine," I told them, seeing as they were still frozen in place like some store manikins with their eyes on me. "She called it the way she saw it. To her, I am a grandmother. No big deal."

Ronin burst out in a nervous laugh. "Sorry. That was just a little too weird, even for me."

Iris let out a long breath. "I need a drink. She better hurry with that wine."

For the next two hours, we ate, we laughed, and we drank. None of it in that order. Getting me out of the house had been exactly what I'd needed, though I didn't realize it until I was sitting in the restaurant, on my second large glass of red wine. At least I could still hold my wine. Things were looking up for Granny Tess.

I might not have been lucky with my recent choices, but I was blessed with friends. Only true friends would try and cheer me up, and I was cheered up. I felt more relaxed than I did when I woke up yesterday with more wrinkles and rolls than your average Shar Pei dog.

"One time, when I was young and foolish," Ronin was saying.

"You're still young and foolish," interjected Iris.

"I sent a picture of... you know..." he glanced down at himself. "To the girl I was dating at the time."

"What's so funny about that?" Iris took a sip of her wine. "You send me those daily," she added, making me laugh.

Ronin pulled his face into a serious mask. "Because her dad saw it."

We all laughed louder because of all the wine we'd drunk.

Ronin leaned back in his chair, looking smug. "Think you can beat that?" he challenged.

I nodded. "I can."

The half-vampire raised a brow. "With what?"

I met Ronin's stare and said, "I'm wearing a diaper."

Ronin threw back his head and laughed. "Good one."

"I'm not kidding."

The half-vampire lost his smile. "I'm not sure what to say to that... is it... *depend*able?"

Iris giggled. "I'm having so much fun. We need to do this like... every week."

I smiled at her, wishing with all my heart that we could but knowing that my expiry date was fast approaching.

I took a sip of my wine and placed my glass on the table. "That would be—"

Marcus walked by outside the restaurant. Next to him was Cameron, one of his deputies. He was also a big, burly man, but he was a few inches shorter than the chief and not as wide. They were deep in conversation, judging by the frowns they both sported.

I smiled as he went by, an impulse reaction, watching his large shoulders sway as he came closer.

But his reaction I was not expecting.

He glanced my way, just a split second, a split second that would have been long enough for the guy you're dating to recognize you.

But he didn't.

His eyes just glazed over me, no recognition, nothing. It was as though he didn't know me. He didn't *see* me, and that hurt like a sonovabitch.

"Hey. Isn't that Marcus?" asked Ronin a few seconds later. "You want me to go get him?"

I stared at my plate, feeling like my pizza was about to come back up and say hello. "No. He's obviously busy with something." It was a hit to the gut, but it was also a wake-up call.

"I know what you're doing," said Iris after a moment.

I looked at her. "Really? What's that?"

"You're trying to distance yourself from him. It's why you haven't answered any of his texts. Don't think I haven't noticed. You think it'll be easier on him when..."

"When I expire?" I answered for her. "Yes, you're right. Why should I drag him along? It wouldn't be fair to him."

No one said anything for a while, and the silence became uncomfortable.

But I wasn't planning on expiring anytime soon.

Not while I still drew breath.

18

After Ronin and Iris dropped me off, and after I repeatedly smacked the half-vampire with Gran's cane yelling that I didn't need his help to walk to my front door, I hobbled down the hallway of Davenport House like a badly oiled clockwork puppet.

The lights from the kitchen were off. The sound of my cane hitting the hardwood floors rang loudly in my ears over the loud beating of my heart that hadn't stopped since I'd seen Marcus.

My body was stiff from sitting for so long. No one told me about that either. It was like an old machine that hadn't been oiled in years, and once you applied the needed oil, it took time to get all the parts going again.

I did my best to keep quiet, but between the loud

thumps of the cane and my feet slapping on the floor, it sounded like I was three people.

Don't even get me started with what my feet looked like. No one could ever prepare you for the yellowing, hard-as-metal toenails. I'd need a chainsaw just to trim them.

I didn't want to alert my aunts, who were probably in their rooms for the night. Beverly was most likely on some hot date.

Every muscle ached as if I had been in a fever. Part of me wanted to go fetch Ruth so she could make me some more of her elixir of youth, but I didn't want her to know what I was planning.

Because if she did, she would try to stop me. They all would. Yes, I was probably doing something stupid. But I was running out of time.

And running out of time trumps stupid.

The image of Marcus walking by the restaurant flashed in my mind's eye. A huge ache of emptiness that had never been there before welled my chest until it felt as though my ribs were about to burst out of my chest. But I didn't have time to feel sorry for myself. I had gotten myself into this mess. I was going to get myself out.

I took a deep breath and stifled my emotions until all I felt was a dull ache. I was going to miss his hot ass if things went sour. And the hot sex. And his hot kisses. And his hot, golden, Greek statue bod. I could keep going...

Still, I wasn't doing this for him. I was doing this for me.

I had two hours before the soul collector came to fetch me. Two hours was plenty enough time to do what I was planning on doing.

Just before entering the kitchen, I made for the room on the left, the potions room. Using Gran's cane, I hit the light switch.

A flutter of excitement rushed through me. It was always a joy stepping into the potions room.

Shelves and racks lined the walls, packed with an assortment of jars with unidentifiable objects. Piled on the shelves and tables sat a vast array of magical ingredients, books, containers, and pouches full of all sorts of herbs, roots, tarot cards, candles, animal bones, crystal balls, pendulums, boxes of chalks, scrying mirrors, and every size of cauldron you could imagine. A center island counter overhung with a rack of drying herbs and flowers was covered in books, shiny copper pots, ceramic spoons, and bowls that were perfect for mixing.

The potions room was for every member of Davenport House, but let's be honest. It was all Ruth's. The air smelled of herbs and dried flowers. It was amazing. No wonder Ruth practically lived here.

At the far end of the room was a patch of floor kept completely clear of all clutter. It was perfect.

I had everything I needed right here for the summoning circle. And with Iris's book *Dark Magic Volume 6: How to Train Your Demon* I'd snatched from her room before going out to eat, I was ready.

So I got to work.

It didn't take long or a genius to realize I was working at the pace of an eighty-year-old woman with severe arthritis, which translated as the speed of a turtle. Going to get the ingredients wasn't a problem, but when I'd been kneeling on the ground perfecting my summoning circle and realized I'd forgotten the candles... that was the problem.

Still, I had my working triangle and circle within twenty minutes. A triangle for the demon and a circle of protection for me because the demon I was about to summon was going to be pissed. My reflexes were not what they were a few days ago. I'd need all the protection I could get.

After I'd written the name Muranda in the middle of the triangle and added the Latin names and symbols, I leaned back to inspect my handiwork.

"Not too shabby, old lady. But it still looks like a four-year-old could have done a better job."

Next, grabbing Iris's book and the magnifying glass I'd found on the island, which I suspected Ruth used for reading, I hauled myself back to my feet using Gran's cane. With some effort, I wobbled into my masterpiece circle and leaned the cane against the nearest wall.

Steadying myself, I balanced the book in my left hand and grabbed the magnifying glass in the other. Working fast, I drew in my will and focused on the incoming energy soaring through me from the elements. I channeled the magic, letting their powers spill into me while I read the incantation.

"I conjure you, Muranda, demon of the Netherworld to be subject to the will of my soul." I took a breath. "I bind you—"

A knock sounded somewhere off in the kitchen.

I jerked.

Marcus. It had to be him. Iris probably called him after I'd shut down during our evening out together. With all that had happened in the last few weeks, I was an emotional mess, barely hanging on.

Seeing Marcus right now was a bad idea. He was a distraction. A sexy as sin one, but still a distraction. With my attention span of a six-year-old, it took all of my concentration just to focus on the task at hand. Plus, I couldn't mess this up. This was my last chance of getting out of this deal with Jack.

Knock. Knock.

"Maybe if I ignore him, he'll go away?"

Knock. Knock. Knock.

"Maybe not."

He was going to wake up the entire house if he didn't stop. Letting out a frustrated breath I dropped my book and magnifying glass on the island, grabbed Gran's cane, and staggered out of the potions room. I shambled across the kitchen and headed toward the back door while butterflies jackhammered the walls of my stomach. I couldn't help it. The chief did that to me.

Darkness stared back at me through the small backdoor window. I couldn't spot him, but seeing as the porch light wasn't on, that didn't come as a surprise.

Knock. Knock. Knock.

I froze, my trembling hand in the air, inches from the doorknob.

The knocking came from *behind* me.

What the hell?

With my heart lodged somewhere in my throat, I shuffled around and stared in the semi-dark kitchen.

I waited as the silence soaked in, broken only by the hum from the refrigerator and the loud thumping of my heart in my ears. "Great. Not only am I losing all motor skills, but I'm also losing my freaking mind."

Knock. Knock. Knock.

"Ah!" I screamed as Gran's cane slipped from my

hand and landed on the hard wood with a loud crash.

The knocking came from the *basement* door.

Did Ruth accidentally lock herself in there? That wasn't possible. The door wouldn't lock for Ruth. Davenport House would never keep her or any of my aunts locked down there.

So who the hell was knocking?

Knock... Knock... Knock!

Composing myself and preparing my favorite power word on my lips, I shuffled my way back across the kitchen to the single white door that led to the basement.

"If this is Ronin's idea of a trick, the half-vampire will never father children."

With a deep breath, I reached out, grabbed the basement's door handle, and yanked it open.

I blinked. "Dad?"

My demon father stood on the basement stairs, wearing a fitted cerulean blue suit and a surprised expression. "Tessa?"

"Dad!"

"Tessa!"

"Will you stop that," I hissed, trying to keep my voice down. "What the hell are you doing here? No —wait—how the hell did you get here?" Demons could not enter Davenport House, so how did my dad end up in the basement?

My father's silver eyes flashed. "There's a gateway. A portal between our two worlds. Between this place and the Netherworld. It's how I was able to send you back when you were in the in-between."

Interesting. "I'd always wondered about that." I frowned at him. "So, any demon can just walk up into our house? That's a little creepy."

"It doesn't work like that. You need a connection to the house."

I frowned. "I have no idea what you're talking about. Come in. And you can tell me all about it."

My father stared at the threshold. "I can't. You have to invite me in. Kind of like with vampires."

I shook my head. "You watch too much TV. Vampires don't need an invitation to enter any house. They go as they please."

"Ah." My father nodded slowly. "Well. Are you going to invite me in? Davenport House will not allow me to step inside if you don't."

"You're already inside," I pointed out.

"Technically, I'm still in the 'crossing.'" He made finger quotes. "I'm not *in*, in."

Still made no sense. "Okay. Fine. I *invite* you in."

My father blinked at me. "You need to be more specific."

"Get your ass inside." I laughed, though he didn't laugh back.

My father frowned. "You sounded just like your mother."

"Enough with the insults, or I'll change my mind." I exhaled loudly. "Okay then. Why don't you tell me how to do it? And make it fast. I need to sit down." The effect of seeing my dad pop up through the basement door had my knees wobbling and about to give way.

"You need to tell the house that I'm allowed in," he said promptly. "That I'm your father and as such, you give me permission to cross over and have access to the house."

Make sense. "House," I said, raising my voice slightly, though I knew I didn't really need to. "This is my father, Obiryn, and I give him permission to cross over and have access to the house."

A sudden surge of energy lifted through and around me, like a gust of warm wind. My skin hummed with power and then it was gone.

I cocked a brow. "Well?"

My father stuck out his right leg, wiggled his foot, and then planted it on the kitchen floor.

"Hah," he exclaimed, touching his chest and arms. "I haven't been obliterated." Looking pleased with himself, my demon father strutted over the threshold and into the kitchen.

Then the basement door shut itself.

"Thanks, House," I whispered, turning back to my dad.

I smiled, even though I had less of a chance at summoning my demon now that father dearest had decided to pay me a visit. Yet somehow, I was really happy to see him. It was... nice.

He glanced around the kitchen, found the light switch, and turned it on. "Nice kitchen. It has that farmhouse vibe with the big farmhouse sink, white cabinets, and white subway tile. The exposed beams are a nice touch."

"You haven't been here before?"

He shook his head. "No. First time."

I thought that was strange since he'd had a relationship with my mother. But then again, my mother was an oddball. Why would she do anything so mundane as to bring her boyfriend to her house to meet her family? She wouldn't.

"Dad," I said as I lowered myself in the nearest chair, the pain in my bones humming to my head. "Don't get me wrong. I'm happy to see you, but what are you doing here?"

My father's silver eyes turned on me and he said, "I know how to make you young again."

19

For a few beats, I just stared at him. "Say that again?"

My father's face lit up as he grabbed a chair from the kitchen table next to me and sat. "I know how to make you young again." His silver eyes shone. "I know how to reverse the aging."

I frowned. "Is this a joke?" Okay, I would not pretend this wasn't the news I'd been waiting for because it was. But could it be real?

My father leaned forward. "It's not a joke. I know how to do it. It's just... I can't believe it took me this long to figure it out."

"How?" I nearly jumped out of my seat to hug him. Though, I'd never actually hugged my father before so that could become awkward really fast.

He clasped his fingers together on his lap. "You

need to remove the bond from all the souls you took. Every last one. Remove the bond, and your life force will be whole again."

I studied him. "Makes sense. How do I do that? And why does it sound like it's not an easy thing to do?" I added, noticing the tension in his voice.

My father ran his hand through his beard, giving away his discomfort. "To break the links with the souls, you'll need to physically do it. What I mean is... you'll need to remove them from the soul catcher device."

I nodded. "That big metal machine he keeps in his locker."

My father smiled. "Exactly." He swallowed and said, "and then you'll have to ingest the souls—"

"Wait—what? No." I made a face. "I'm not eating souls."

"It's not eating per se. It's more like a transfer. The souls need to pass through you to sever the part of your own soul that's linked to them. To remove the bond."

I shifted in my seat. "Okay. Still gross. But I get it." If it would reverse my premature aging, I'd do it.

My father sat up straight in his chair, his silver eyes roving over the kitchen. "And, if it all goes well..."

"If it all goes well? You're not sure?"

He looked at me for a long time. "Theoretically,

you'll be just as you were before you took on the job with the soul collector."

I frowned at him. "Theoretically? You mean, you don't know if it'll work?"

"It'll work."

I gave him a dubious look. "Fine. I'll try it." It was better than summoning another demon. He was still eyeing the kitchen like he thought it should be a showroom or something.

I thought about telling him that Jack had screwed me over with the contract, that I wasn't in his service for a month but rather for the rest of my life. But I didn't want to get into it right now. One step at a time. Besides, he looked so happy to have found a way to help me. I didn't want to ruin the moment.

"You said you've never been here before? In Davenport house? So, where did you and my mother spend time together?"

My father leaned back in his chair and crossed his legs at the knee. "We usually met up at night, had dinner. Either at my place or a restaurant. She had such a wonderful laugh, your mother. I do miss it."

"Your place?" My demon dad was full of surprises. "You mean you have a house here? On this side of the earthly planes?"

"Had," he corrected. "It was sold years ago."

Irritation gripped me. "You can travel on this

plane? Why haven't I seen you before? Why have you waited all this time to show yourself?" My voice rose with anger. I could have used a real dad back when I was a teenager. I'd always assumed he'd been trapped somehow, and that his only means to communicate were through the ley lines. The notion that he wasn't made me want to have House throw him back out the basement door.

He was silent for a long moment. "My earthly travel privileges were revoked. I can no longer journey to this world. Not if I don't want to die my true death."

"They can do that?" I still didn't know how the whole Netherworld hierarchy worked.

"They can. Portals like this one," he added, glancing around the kitchen, "are the exception. But only a few are left in your world, and you can't cross over if the other side is closed to you. I took a chance that you might be here tonight."

"But why? Why would they keep you from coming here?"

A sad smile reached his eyes. "You. Because I had you with your mother. Half-demon offspring is a big no-no within the demon community." He raised his hands and make a gesture. "It's *taboo*. I was found out, and I was banished from the mortal world, in a way." A smile worked its way back on his face. "But ley lines aren't recognized as a real source of power and magic in the Netherworld. They didn't know I knew how to use them. So I kept quiet. Hoping that one day…"

"I'd use them." I stared at my father. "Did my mother know? About the ley lines?"

He nodded. "She did."

"And she never told me." It was hard not to despise the woman at this very moment.

"Don't be angry with her," he said.

I snorted. "That's like asking the cat not to gut the mouse with its claws."

"There's still so much you don't know about where I'm from. Your mother was only trying to protect you."

"By lying to me."

"Hiding some truths."

"That's the same as lying."

We both started laughing. Yeah, it was obvious we shared the same DNA.

The sound of someone approaching dragged my attention toward the hallway.

"Tessa? Do you not realize that your voice carries all the way to our bedrooms?"

Dolores stepped into the kitchen, wearing a long light blue nightgown, a sleep mask on the top of her head, and a deep scowl as she looked from me to my dad.

"Sorry," I began just as Beverly waltzed into the

kitchen in a pink, short sexy nightie under a cherry red kimono.

"Oh! Hello," said Beverly, as she moved her hips and came to stand close to my father, her red boa mule slippers clacking on the hard wood. "Tessa? Who's this perfect specimen of a man?" she purred. "It's rude not to introduce your guest."

"It's rude to invite strangers in during the middle of the night and not tell us," scolded Dolores.

Oh, boy. "Ladies," I said, preparing myself, "this is my father, Obiryn." It occurred to me that I didn't know his last name. Did demons have surnames?

My father stood up, looking like the perfect gentleman. "It's my pleasure to meet Amelia's sisters. I've heard so much about all of you."

"Your father!" Ruth came running into the kitchen like a tiny hurricane of white hair and pink and white polka dot pajamas with Minnie Mouse's face on them.

She halted a foot from my father with a slightly open mouth and eyes so wide they looked like they might pop out.

"You must be Ruth," said my father.

Ruth jumped back and clapped her hands excitedly. "He knows my name! Oh, this is so much fun. Try to guess Beverly's name next."

"Excuse her," said Dolores, shaking her head. "She forgot to take her meds."

After a moment, Dolores came forward, worry etching her brow. "I'm glad to finally meet you, Obiryn. And thank you for saving our Tessa. But how is it possible that you're in my kitchen? You're a demon. Demons can't enter Davenport House."

"About that," I said before he could answer. I quickly told them what my father had just revealed about the connection to the house since he was my father, and my permitting him to enter.

"You know," said Beverly, a hand on my father's arm. "Amelia and I are only two years apart." Her voice went suddenly husky. "But I'm better than her in... *everything*," she added suggestively.

Dolores shook her head. "Leave the poor man alone, Beverly."

Beverly gave her sister a frown. "I haven't done anything to him... *yet*," she added with a smile.

A flash of annoyance crossed Dolores's face. "This is going to be a long night."

"I'll make some coffee." Ruth moved to the counter and filled the coffee pot with water just as Dolores came around the table and took the seat facing me.

My father gave me a tight smile and sat back down in his chair. I was glad he was here, not only for me, but this was a chance for my aunts to get to know him. I could tell they liked him already.

I checked the clock on my phone and my heart

sank. "I better get going. It's almost ten." Part of me wanted to stay here with my aunts and father. But the winning part wanted to get my life back—all those precious years Jack had stolen from me.

"I can't wait until you're finished with that," commented Dolores. "Only a week and a half left. Right?"

"Right," I lied, my insides squirming. I was hoping my new face wouldn't show my guilt.

"And then we'll fix you back up. Make you young again," said Ruth, as she came around and placed a steaming cup of coffee on the table for my father followed by one for Dolores.

I met my father's eyes, and his face went straight in understanding. I let out a sigh in relief, grateful he'd keep quiet about our plan. The last thing I needed was to worry my aunts. If it worked, great. If not, I'd be back to square one.

I went to stand up but then stopped and looked at my father. "Do you go back to your... home the same way you came in?"

My father smiled. "Yes. But if it's all right with you and your aunts, I should like to stay for a little while."

"Sure, if that's what you want." I wasn't sure if he was asking to get my permission or House's permission.

"Don't worry," said Dolores, mistaking the hesitation and unease on my face. "We won't eat him."

"I can't promise anything." Beverly smiled, her hands on the backrest of my father's chair, staring at him like he was sex on two legs.

"Okay then. I'll see you all later." Having managed to pull myself up on my own, with only the help of Gran's cane, I hobbled down the hall, my pulse hammering.

For the first time, I was anxious for my night shift. Not because of the additional years that would be knocked off my body from the souls I'd collect tonight but because this time, things would go my way.

This time, I was going to get my life back.

20

Just like the night before, Jack had worked me into exhaustion to get a total of thirty-five contracted souls in one night. I was actually happy to be back in the in-between, which was saying a lot as my stiff body rebelled against my every step.

Jack's version of a new protective suit was a multicolored wool shawl. Apparently, my body shape was all wrong. His words. Not mine.

He said it would help keep me "fresh" longer. It did help, somewhat. I didn't feel as weak and nauseated whenever I collected a new soul. If we had stopped at ten souls, maybe the shawl would have been worthwhile, but Jack kept pushing for more. The more souls I collected, the more of myself disappeared and the frailer I grew as my body crumbled, like a beat-up old station wagon, rotting away in the junkyard.

The only thing that kept me going was my father's plan. Now my plan.

After the newly collected souls were safely inside the soul containment machine and the newly signed contracts hidden away inside Jack's jacket, I stood there waiting and contemplating how I was going to distract the demon long enough to test my father's theory.

"Well, time for you to get some shut-eye," said Jack, extending his arm out like we were about to take a stroll in the park.

Shit. "I think I'll stay a while. Might as well get used to my new life, seeing as this is going to be it, for the rest of it." I flashed him the most honest smile I could muster.

Jack looked pleased. "Excellent. I knew you'd come around. Well, you can stay for as long as you like. Make yourself comfortable." The demon spun around and walked off into the darkness.

Strange how he thought I could actually make myself comfortable in this nothingness. I had no idea where he was going since I couldn't see anything beyond the darkness that surrounded this place. Nor did I know when he'd be back.

So I waited.

The animal familiars were nowhere to be found.

I hadn't seen them for a few days, which worried me. I'd been meaning to ask Jack about them, but with him gone, I guessed it would have to wait.

When I thought I'd finally waited long enough, I moved to the front of the machine and searched for a button or anything that would serve as a purging sort of device.

Next to one of the compartments were two buttons—one red, one green—and a lever. Bingo.

Glancing over my shoulder and seeing only darkness, I whirled back around, lifted my gnarled hand, and pressed on the red button. Nothing. Then I pressed on the green button. Still nothing. Finally, I grabbed the lever and pulled it down. Then pushed up. And a big nothing.

"Maybe I should be pressing on the buttons and then pulling on the lever?" I whispered to myself.

Frustrated and trying to keep my wits about me, I reached out again and pressed on the green button before I pulled down on the lever.

You guessed it, nothing.

Trying not to panic, I pressed the red button and pulled on the lever.

Not so much as a hum or a click sounded from the machine.

"Damn you!" I kicked it, feeling a wave of desperation hit me until I feared I might collapse.

"What are you doing?" came a voice from behind me.

I jerked and tried to turn around, but my knees had locked, and I fell.

My cane hit the floor first. Next came me. Searing pain flared up in my right hip. I used my hands to stop my fall and felt something crack in both wrists. Wonderful. I clenched my teeth as my entire body reverberated in pain to my skull.

"What are you doing on the floor?" asked the same voice.

I twisted my head and stared up into the face of a black cat. "You owe me a new hip. And two new kneecaps."

Hildo laughed. "Barbara used to say that. She was my witch back in the seventies." The cat padded over and sniffed my face. "You've aged. Like, a lot."

"Tell me something I don't know." I shifted my weight and hissed as more pain came flooding in, but I managed to push myself to a half-decent sitting position. "I think I'll just sit here for a while. Until my body stops throbbing."

Hildo leaped onto my lap. "You still haven't told me what you were doing to the soul collector's machine. Why'd you kick it?"

Apparently, cat familiars were just as curious as any regular house cat. "Well, if you must know, I was testing a theory," I said as I stroked the top of the cat's head, finding it really soothing.

"Which is?" asked the cat as he started to purr.

"That if I released the souls trapped in there—the ones linked to me—it would break the connection and I'd get those parts of me back, making me young again."

The cat cocked his head to the side. "It didn't work."

A depressed, frustrated sigh emitted from me. "Thanks for the tip." I ran my fingers through his fur. Seeing that he closed his eyes in delight, I kept going. "Where were you guys? I haven't seen you in a while. I thought something had happened to you."

"In hiding," answered the cat. "We're hoping the soul collector will forget about us. He's been really distracted lately. So far, I think it's working."

"Because he's been *working* me," I grumbled.

"Sorry." Hildo lay on my lap and stretched out his limbs.

I smiled down at the cat. If this was going to be my new normal, maybe it wouldn't be so bad to be stuck with him here. At least I'd have a friend.

"Right behind the left ear, please," instructed the cat.

I laughed and obliged. "Yes, sir."

Hildo purred even more loudly. "You know, all

that work he's doing, making you get all those souls... I don't think it's going to get her back."

I frowned. "Get who back?"

"His wife."

My hand froze. "The soul collector has a wife?"

"He does."

"And where is she?" I asked.

"The reaper has her."

I tried to do a double-take, but instead, I gave myself whiplash. Okay. This was all kinds of weird.

I shook my head and stopped petting the cat. "You're not making any sense. What's going on? What do you know? Tell me."

Hildo opened his eyes and turned to look at me, yellow eyes gleaming. "To summarize, our soul collector took something that didn't belong to him. A soul. A soul that was promised to the reaper. To his credit, the soul collector didn't know this. He took it and sold it, though. When the reaper found out, he was pissed. So, he took the soul collector's wife as payment."

"Holy crap." I thought about it. "And a reaper is more powerful than a soul collector? I thought they were the same thing?" Goes to show how unknowledgeable I was.

The cat's tail whipped on either side of him. "They're not. Reapers are angels."

"Angels?" I asked, surprised. "Oh, right. The

angels of death and all that. I've heard the stories. Just never thought they were true."

"Well, they are. Reapers are responsible for escorting souls to the afterlife, and soul collectors steal them."

I scratched Hildo under his chin, and he closed his eyes in pleasure. "You're one smart kitty. How come you know all this stuff?"

The cat cocked a brow. "I've been around for over a hundred years. I might not look it, but I'm a hundred and eleven."

"Happy birthday." I smiled.

Hildo turned his yellow eyes on me again. "A reaper is like a king, and a soul collector is more like a working-class mortal with a nine-to-five job. He's been trying to get her back ever since. He thinks offering as many souls as possible will get her back. So far, it hasn't worked."

"It explains why he's been so adamant about getting all those souls before the end of the week. He was trying to buy her back with souls. Why he's been pushing me so hard."

"Yup."

I dipped my head. "And the reaper won't give her back?"

"No. He won't. He's enjoying seeing Jack squirm. I think he's hurting her. The wife, I mean."

I didn't like Jack. I liked him as much as I liked a

leech. I liked the leech better. But I hated this reaper even more. "I can't believe I'm saying this, but I kind of feel sorry for Jack."

"I don't," hissed the cat, his nails clipping through my sweatpants and into my skin. "He put us in here. He did this. He did this to you."

"I know."

"I want to claw his eyes out."

"Me too. If I had claws."

We laughed at that, and it felt both eerie and good to be laughing in another plane of existence.

"What's going on here?" Jack had appeared from the darkness like a Houdini from hell.

I looked up at the demon. "Enjoying quality time with my buddy here."

Jack frowned, staring at the cat. "Ah, yes. The familiars. I had forgotten about them."

Hildo stiffened and I felt like an ass now. If I hadn't been kicking the machine, the cat would have stayed hidden and out of sight of the demon. Great.

I wrapped my arms protectively around the cat. "Is there something you want?" I asked, hoping to distract him from the familiars.

"Yes." Jack straightened the sleeves of his jacket. "I'm here to tell you to go home and get some rest. I'll need you to be in tiptop shape tomorrow."

"Why's that?"

"We have fifty-three souls to collect." He raised

his thin hand. "I know. I know. It's more than you're accustomed to, but I have no choice in the matter."

I opened my mouth to protest but stopped. Now that I knew, I could see how jittery the demon was, the nervous twitching of his fingers, the tension in his shoulders, the way his eyes flicked everywhere at once. He was clearly on the verge of a massive meltdown. He was desperate to get his wife back.

And then I had a lightbulb moment.

Foolish? Maybe. Insane? Probably.

"If I can get your wife back, will you break our contract?" I blurted before I could stop myself. Hildo turned to look up at me, but I kept my focus on the demon.

Jack froze, his face expressionless as his white eyes rolled over me. "Who told you about my wife?"

"News travels fast in the in-between," I told him, and I saw his eyes flick down to the cat. "If I can get her back from the reaper, will you destroy that contract?"

The demon hunched his shoulders, and I saw real pain on his face. "I appreciate you trying, Tessa. But he will not give her back to you, a mere mortal. I have a plan in place to get her back."

"Is it working?"

"Not yet." Jack clenched and unclenched his fingers. "It's a work in progress. One cannot simply ask a reaper to give something back."

"Not even your wife?" When he didn't answer, I added, "And with this plan, he'll give her back?" When he said nothing, I pressed. "You're not sure he will. Are you? I can see it written all over your face. Listen. If *I* can get her back, will you destroy my contract?"

This time Jack looked at me as though he just saw me for the first time. "You think you can? How?"

"I have my ways. I can be persuasive." I picked up Hildo and placed him on the ground. Next, I grabbed Gran's cane and dragged myself up. I was bent, but at least I was up. I met the demon's eyes and said, "But I'm going to need some time off."

Jack's hairless brow reached the bridge of his nose. "How much time?"

I took the fact that he didn't object as a good sign. "Maybe a day or two. Enough time to find the reaper and negotiate. Do we have a deal?"

Jack pressed his lips together. "If you can get her back to me... yes. Yes, you have a deal."

"And the familiars," I added, glancing down at the black cat at my feet. Hildo let out a meow and rubbed against my leg. "All of them. I bring you back your wife, and we all go free. No tricks. No funny business. No fine print crap. Deal?" I held out my hand.

Jack stared at it for a moment, and just when I

thought he wouldn't, he stepped forward and we shook hands.

"Deal," said the demon, watching me curiously.

I grinned. "Excellent," I said, realizing I had just sounded a lot like the soul collector. I felt great, though. More than great.

Because now *I* was back in business.

21

According to my new bestie Hildo, the reaper owned a nightclub in downtown Boston called, you guessed it, GRIM. Not very original, but whatever. I wasn't the language police, and he went by the name Malak.

From Hollow Cove to Boston was a four-hour drive. By ley line, it was a few minutes at best, but the last time I rode a ley line, I nearly lost control of the lines and my bladder. I could have died if my father hadn't shown up.

Not to mention that I needed all of my magical mojo left to face this reaper. I had no idea what to expect. It wasn't every day one faced an angel, the angel of death no less. And if a soul collector demon feared him, you could bet I was probably going to be scared shitless too. I couldn't risk getting there weak and shaky from using a ley line. First appearances were important. I needed every drop of witch magic in me.

Which explained why I'd been sitting in the front seat of a burgundy Jeep Grand Cherokee for nearly four hours, enduring Marcus's constant stares and forced pleasant conversations. The guy was worried about me. It was nice that he cared, but the more he treated me like a frail old woman, the more I wanted to knock him over the head with Gran's cane.

"You'd think there'd be more leg room in your Jeep," stated Ronin, who was sitting right behind Marcus, and I heard the leather squeak as he shifted in his seat. "At the price they're going for now. And what's this?" I turned my head and saw him move his hand over the door. "Is this plastic?" he laughed.

"Your beamer has some plastic interior elements too," commented Marcus, the muscles of his jaw twitching and a frown on his face as he kept his eyes on the road.

Ronin made a face. "Dude, I don't drive plastic cars."

Iris, sitting next to him with Dana, her DNA album of curses, inside a cloth bag on her lap, punched him on the shoulder. "Give it a rest. Who cares what it's made of? As long as it gets us where we need to go."

Both Ronin and Marcus let out grunts of disapproval.

I rolled my eyes. Men and their cars—a bond I'd never understand.

When I'd woken earlier this afternoon, I'd been surprised to find Ronin seated next to Iris at the kitchen table with my aunts. Marcus was leaning against the kitchen counter, his arms crossed over his large chest and a tiny smile across his face as he listened to something Ruth was telling him as she stirred something in a pot on the stove.

I'd felt a surge of butterflies fluttering in my stomach when our eyes had met. Staring at those mesmerizing gray eyes, I'd forgotten about my eighty-year-old exterior. Eyes like that could make you forget a lot of things, like underwear. But those feelings quickly died when his expression turned to worry and then something like the look someone gives you when you tell them that you have an incurable disease.

At that moment, feeling even more miserable, I came clean about the soul collector to everyone—about how he'd tricked me to become his slave for the rest of my existence and finally my plan to meet up with the reaper. My aunts weren't thrilled, but this was my only shot. I had to do something quickly before I turned into dust.

And when Marcus, Iris, and Ronin volunteered

to come with me, I was surprised yet relieved because I was going to need some serious backup.

What was more surprising was when Marcus had let out that he knew the reaper.

"You know him?" I'd asked as I sipped on my coffee.

"Long story," he acknowledged, avoiding my eyes, his posture stiff with tension. "I'll tell you on the way there. I'll be back in two hours to pick you up." And with that, the chief had left.

My chest felt like it was caving in, but I had to focus on getting my life back. If my crazy plan worked, I'd have lots of time to make it up to him.

I pulled my gaze back to Marcus. "Are you going to tell me about the reaper now? We're almost in Boston. It would be great to get a little heads up for what I can expect."

"Yeah. I want to know this too," came Ronin's voice from the back. "What'd you do? You must have done something?"

I spun my head in Ronin's direction and scowled at him.

"What?" The half-vampire shrugged. "It's a valid question."

"All I could find on the internet was the same old angel of death stuff," I added, turning to look back at the chief. "They reap the souls of mortals and guide them to the afterlife. That kind of thing. My aunts weren't much help either. So if you know anything, now would be a great time to share."

Marcus was silent for a long moment. He kept his eyes on the road as he said, "I met the reaper about twelve years ago. He's not what you'd expect."

"He likes to dress as a woman?" I asked, making Ronin laugh by trying to lighten the mood. It didn't work.

Still frowning, Marcus let out a long sigh. "He's more of a mob boss. He rules all of Boston's paranormal community."

Ronin whistled. "Is he more like Vito Corleone or Tony Soprano?"

I shifted in my seat, trying to ease some of the pain in my hip but only managing to make it worse. "But he's an angel. Shouldn't he be with the other angels? Watching over the humans like they're supposed to?" I cringed on the inside at my own ignorance. I sounded like a human, not a witch. I wasn't going to lie. I knew next to nothing about angels. And reapers even less.

Marcus finally looked at me. "Reapers are powerful angels. They're right alongside the archangels in terms of strength." He flicked his eyes back to the road. "But what sets them apart is their close connection to the humans and the mortal world. As long as they have access to souls, which he does, they can stay here as long as they want. Malak claimed Boston as his territory in the early eighteenth century. Nothing happens in the paranormal community without his knowledge and approval."

"I'm guessing it won't be a breeze to bargain with him. Right?"

"It won't. He's dangerous. Smart. And everyone is afraid of him. Forget what you know about angels," Marcus kept going. "This guy is not all glowing with white wings."

"Don't forget the halo," interjected Ronin.

Marcus's grip on the wheel tightened. "This guy is terrifying. He's bad, Tessa. The soul collector is like a child to this guy."

"That's just great." I swallowed hard, trying to ignore the increase of my beating heart but failing. "So how did you get involved with him? How did you meet him?" I asked, my jaw clenching at the pain in my knees from sitting for so long.

A strange look flashed on his face that appeared to be embarrassment. "Twelve years ago, I went to Boston with my cousins. I was young and stupid. Throw in hormones and a pretty female shifter, and I got into a fight with another male shifter. Turns out the shifter woman I was with had a boyfriend."

"Huh. So who won?" I was not surprised another man's woman would throw herself at a young Marcus.

Marcus smiled. "I did." The smile on his face

melted away. "I'd had too much to drink and I went too far. I nearly killed him. I was a stupid kid trying to show off in front of all the women. If my cousins hadn't pulled me off of him, I probably would have killed him."

I rolled my eyes over his beautiful, perfect features. "Let me guess, the reaper found out."

The chief nodded. "And his crew came to find me. They took me to him."

"What happened?" I asked, seeing his posture holding a fit of repressed anger. The utter silence in the back told me that Iris and Ronin were hanging on his every word. They wanted to hear this too.

Marcus's face turned dark with hatred. "He let me live," he said, and I knew he was holding something back. "I was lucky."

My stomach was in knots. I could tell there was a lot more to the story. He was hiding something, but I also knew he wouldn't share it. Well, not now with Ronin and Iris. I made a mental note to ask about it when we were alone. If that ever happened again.

By the time we hit downtown Boston, the digital clock on the Jeep's dashboard read 8:14 p.m. I was starting to feel more jittery and nervous about meeting the reaper. Would he even see me? What did I know of mob bosses? I took my knowledge of mob bosses from the *Godfather* movies I'd seen years ago, which I barely remembered. Add the paranormal element, and I still had nothing.

Too late to turn around now. Besides, I was running out of time. The longer I stayed in this body, the shorter my lifespan became. I needed to do this now.

"Here it is." Marcus rolled the steering wheel toward a free space next to the curb, parked, and killed the engine.

I followed Marcus's gaze and looked out the window. Along the street stood a row of several cramped buildings. Nestled in the middle was a structure of gleaming black stone, metal, and iron. Above a single black door, the name GRIM was illuminated in orange lights.

A thick wall of a man whose clothes could barely contain the muscles on him stood smack in front of the door. His gaze was fixed to Marcus's Jeep. I had a feeling he was going to be a giant pain in my ass.

"You think those are real muscles?" came Ronin's voice near my ear.

Iris laughed. "Your body's just fine."

"What's that supposed to mean?" asked the half-vampire.

I couldn't catch Iris's response as I pushed open the door with my foot. Then I grabbed the doorframe and hauled myself out, wobbling for a moment, just as Marcus came around.

He held out his arm. "Here. Let me help."

"I'm fine." My mood souring, I yanked Gran's cane from the floor of the Jeep and steadied myself with it.

"I'm just trying to help," said the chief, a tiny, irritated frown twitching on his forehead.

"I know." I let out a breath. "But if I want to appear like a badass old witch who can hold her own, I can't have you cater to me like that. I can't look weak. Not with what I'm planning." I looked across the street to the bouncer, who was still watching us.

"Okay." Marcus flashed me a smile that nearly had me forget why I was standing in downtown Boston for a second. "Ladies first," he gestured with his hand.

With Iris and Ronin next to me on my right and Marcus on my left, we crossed the wet, snow-covered street and headed straight for the club—well, the wall of a man, really.

His dark eyes stayed glued to Marcus, probably pegging him for his biggest challenge. He was probably right.

I planted myself about two feet in front of the bouncer. "We're here to see Malak," I told him, wrinkling my nose at the stench of wet dog. Yup. This guy was a werewolf. It explained why he was wearing just a black T-shirt and jeans in the middle of winter.

Werewolves didn't feel the cold like the rest of us mere mortals.

The bouncer crossed his arms over his enormous chest in a show of strength, flexing his muscles as he did. His eyes remained on Marcus, who had that little wicked smile on his face. Great. He thought this was amusing.

I straightened, which was barely noticeable, and stuck out my chest. Didn't know why I did that since the girls were somewhere around my belly button.

"I have business to discuss with your boss, Malak," I continued. "Are you going to make an old lady wait outside?" Yes, I was going to play that card.

"This is a private club," he said, his voice low and rumbly like the grinding of rocks. "No outsiders allowed," he added, his eyes leaving Marcus and flicking over to Ronin while still not looking at me. "Especially half-breeds."

I heard Ronin's intake of breath. The bouncer didn't so much as look at me or give any sign that I was an actual person standing here.

My mood blackened.

I tapped into the elements, flicked my right wrist with Gran's cane, and growled, "Inflitus."

A blast of kinetic force lashed out from my outstretched hands and struck the bouncer square in the chest. It threw him back like a cannonball of blazing force. He hit the door, causing it to explode off its hinges and disappear with him somewhere inside the club, leaving a cloud of dust and debris.

Whoops.

I'd barely touched my will with that power word, yet the magic that had soared out of me was much more potent than when I'd used it before. I stared curiously at the cane in my hand. Either Gran's cane was some sort of magical conduit or my magic had quadrupled with my age.

Now that was all kinds of awesome.

As the power word's energy slipped out of me, I shivered, but I was surprised that it hadn't drained me or left me more exhausted than I already felt.

"That was amazing," commented Ronin, reading my mind. "You've got some wicked grandma witch power."

I rolled my shoulders. "I'm amazing."

Marcus stepped over some debris and stood at the hole that used to be a door. He looked at me with a smile and said, "Did you have to break the door down and take the bouncer with it?"

I shrugged. "Old lady hormones," I said, not knowing if that was even a thing. But what I did know was that Malak would know we were here.

With Iris laughing next to me, we all followed Marcus inside. We entered a shadowed entryway with an orange light overhead. Some sort of dark classical music was playing a soaring tune with sadness at its core. The air was stuffy, full of cigarette smoke and the stink of booze, yet I could still feel the familiar pull of paranormal energies and something else.

The air grew tight with some sort of energy I'd never felt before, a power that grated against my witch senses like the claws from some hungry beast waiting to strike at me from the darkness. The reaper's power.

When we reached the spot where the bouncer lay motionless on the ground, Iris rushed past me, knelt next to the werewolf, and with the smallest scissors I'd ever seen, started to snip some of his hair.

"Is he still alive?" I asked. If I'd killed him, that wouldn't go so well with the reaper.

"He's alive." Iris pulled Dana out of her bag and carefully placed her newly cut werewolf hair on one of the pages. She caught me staring and said, "I was running low of werehair," like that explained her compulsion for DNA extracts.

"I've always had a thing for the weird ones," said Ronin, a smile on his face.

Moving on.

The hallway opened up to a larger room with a low ceiling. Orange and blue lights played over a small dance floor. We passed a bar to our right as we sauntered through. Bottles of beer and mixed drinks littered the bar top. I glanced around at the surrounding men and women sitting at the bar. Not one glanced in our direction as we crossed the empty dance floor.

We passed the dance floor and followed the chief to a door at the back, where he knocked twice and waited. The door swung open and revealed a beautiful woman with short red hair. Her porcelain skin was covered in tattoos, and her green eyes flicked briefly on all of us for a moment before she stepped aside and let us in.

We entered a game-like room with oak paneling and gray carpets. The few windows were covered with a thick black fabric. A group of paranormals sat around a blackjack table and a poker table. The clatter of chips and muffled voices had my heart hammering. About a dozen other paranormals—a mix of vampires, weres, a few trolls, and my favorite, faeries, if my instincts were right—sat or lounged comfortably on sofas and chairs. They all had something in common. Their eyes all narrowed, full of hatred and anger.

A small female sat on the floor next to one of the couches. She had delicate, pixie-like features with a mane of white hair past her waist. A rhinestone bikini was the only cover for her thin frame, and the light shimmered on a metal chain around her neck. She looked sick with dark circles showing under her pale skin. I knew, without a doubt, this was Jack's wife. And I also knew as a demon, the air from our world was slowly killing her. She couldn't stay here in this world much longer.

The group of paranormals didn't have me on edge nearly as much as the army of skeletons.

Yes, skeletons. With sightless eyes and pale white bones, they stood against the far walls with swords and daggers, like soldiers at attention, waiting for a command from their leader.

A large male stood from the couch behind Jack's wife. He was tall, trim, and muscular, with ebony skin and a shaved head, his grooming immaculate. He was handsome, with a perfectly sculpted face, and he wore a gunmetal gray suit that fit snugly over his athletic physique, giving off the impression of a serious businessman. Everything about this man radiated authority. My breath caught, and it took every bit of my control to stay where I was.

He wasn't radiating with a golden glow or a halo, but he was radiating something. Power. A crap load of it.

The air around him cackled with energy, and a mountain of power hung around him in a thin haze. I'd felt the same strange power when we walked in.

He was mesmerizing—lethal, beautiful, and merciless. He looked more like a vampire than an angel. But what did I know? I'd never met an angel.

He looked to be in his forties, but who knew how old he truly was? A thousand? Two thousand?

He watched me with eyes that were so dark I couldn't tell if they were brown or black. His dominance was nearly palpable. And then he gave me a smile that had the hairs on the back of my neck standing up and making my pulse quicken.

The reaper's dark eyes focused on me and he said, "Are you the idiot who broke my door?"

Yup. This was going to be fantastic.

22

I swallowed, waiting a few seconds for my mouth muscles to work. "That was an accident. Sorry about that." Not a total lie. I had only planned on removing the bouncer. The door had gotten in the way.

I wondered how he knew it was me. It could just as easily have been Marcus or Ronin who'd kicked the door down.

"I can smell the magic on you," said the reaper, as though he'd read my thoughts. His voice was rough and commanding like the crack of thunder.

O-o-o-kay. Creepy as hell.

I leaned on my cane. "Thanks." *Thanks?* Here I went again with the word vomit when I got nervous.

"What are two witches, a half-vampire and a wereape doing in my city without my permission?"

snarled the reaper, the air around him ringing with power.

"This is going great," muttered Ronin.

"I'll take care of it," I whispered back. Clearing my throat, I spoke to the reaper again, "I have a business proposal. See..."

But the reaper's attention suddenly moved to Marcus, his expression unreadable. "I thought I told you if you ever set foot in my city again... I would kill you."

"Oh, shit, this is bad. This is bad," muttered Ronin and I felt him stiffen next to me.

I whipped my head at Marcus. "You didn't think of mentioning that part?"

Marcus shrugged. "I forgot."

"Right..." I pulled my gaze back on the reaper. "Look. I don't know all the details about what happened with Marcus all those years ago, but he's here because of me. I asked him to come."

"Wereapes are the most primal of you shifters. You don't take well to orders," continued the reaper. "It's why I don't have them in my city. It's why I'm going to kill you." He snapped his fingers.

The skeletons, maybe about twenty of them, pushed off the wall and came forward at an alarming speed. The sound of bones popping and grinding was both horrifying and disturbingly familiar to my own.

"Malak! Wait!" I shouted, my voice surprisingly loud.

The reaper stared at me, clearly annoyed, but it had worked. His skeleton army had halted.

"Can I call you Malak? Yeah? Great," I prattled on. "Listen, I'm here for her," I said, pointing with Gran's cane to the tiny female demon on the floor. "I'm here for the soul collector's wife."

Malak turned his head and stared at Jack's wife, who cowered, and then he snapped his attention back to me. "I can smell the demon stink on you. I can see what it's done to your beauty. Made you old. Made you weak."

"I'm not weak," I snapped.

Malak smiled at that. "And why is that, witch? What do you want with the demon's wife? I should think you'd want her dead. Look what it's cost you."

"I made a deal with him that I would bring her back safely."

Malak laughed, and it wasn't musical or beautiful. It was dark, nasty, and terrifying. In a blur, he twisted, grabbed the metal chain off the floor, and yanked.

Jack's wife went sprawling forward on the ground, her hands around her throat, as she coughed, trying to breathe.

Bastard.

"The soul collector took something of mine... so

I took something of his." He pulled on the chain again, and the demon female stumbled forward. Malak smiled at the horror on my face. "She's not for sale."

"Everything's for sale." I stood my ground, knowing this celestial being could most probably end me with a snap of his fingers, but I was betting he was the greedy type. Why else settle here in the mortal realm, surrounded by people to mount his ego.

Marcus's attention snapped to mine, his brow pinched in worry. He knew we came to make a deal or to try and convince the reaper to hand over Jack's wife. Only I hadn't given the chief all of the details because I didn't think he'd agree if he knew what I was going to propose.

Malak smiled, his hand still wrapped around the chain. "What do you have in mind?"

Gotcha. "Is there something you desire? Is there something, anything, you want but you can't have?" When I saw his eyes widen just a tad, I knew I had him.

"And you can get that for me?"

"I can." I had no freaking clue what he was talking about.

Iris leaned in and whispered. "We can still make a run for it. I have a shield hex that can cover us while we run."

"I've got this," I told her and she leaned back.

Without letting go of the chain, Malak made his way back to his couch and sat. I waited while he lit a cigar. He leaned back and crossed his legs at the knee. "Now that you've mentioned it, I require something of great value. Something I can't reach. Something tied with magic beyond this world that only a powerful witch can retrieve."

"That's me," I declared.

Malak laughed. "You? A powerful witch?"

At that, his entourage of paranormals cronies laughed, which set my blood on fire.

"You look more like a beaten old woman whose body is slowly losing control," Malak mocked, and it was all I could do to keep from spitting in his face.

I nodded. "You're right. I have gas more times than I'd like to admit and you can forget about bladder control, 'cause those days are gone. I might be a spandex, diaper-wearing old witch, but that doesn't change the power that runs in my veins."

"She's the most powerful witch I've ever known," interjected Iris, stepping forward. "You laugh because you only see her exterior. Her shell. But her shell is not easily broken. She's tough—a lot tougher than the lot of you."

The reaper's attention snapped to the Dark witch and I cringed. I appreciated her solidarity, but I didn't want her to be turned into a pile of ashes either.

Malak frowned at Iris's bag, and I had a feeling he could see Dana.

"Thank you, for that wonderful rendition, darling." Ronin grabbed Iris and yanked her back, shielding her with his body. "I think he gets it."

Using Gran's cane, I hobbled a step forward, my pulse speeding with excitement. "I'm that witch. The one who can get you what you want." I hoped he couldn't see through the bullshit. "So? What is it?"

Malak watched me. "My scythe."

I cocked a brow. "That's a sharp curved-like sword that cuts grass and wheat. Right?"

"That's not its purpose, but yes." Malak puffed on his cigar. "It was taken from me a few centuries ago. No matter how many times I've tried to get it back, I can't."

"Because it's protected with spells and hexes and wards?" I guessed.

Malak's dark eyes met mine. "Yes. I've had many strong mages and sorcerers try over the years, but they've all failed me. You think you can do better?"

"I do."

The same woman who'd answered the door came around Malak and gave him a drink of honey-colored liquid. He took a sip as she moved away. He leaned forward, his eyes focused on me, and I could see the deep desire he had for this object. "Well, witch. If you can bring me back my scythe, I will give you the soul collector's wife."

It pissed me off that he didn't care to know my name, but we couldn't have it all. It just went to show what kind of arrogant bastard he was. Even Jack knew my real name.

Okay, not so bad. So far so good. "Where is it?"

"In the pyramid of Menkaure."

"That's in Egypt. Right? Giza?" I remembered reading about those three pyramids years ago.

Malak's eyes widened. "That's right."

"I'll get it for you," I told him, seeing him smile in smug satisfaction. Seeing an opening, feeling bold and brash in my *older* years, I added. "But I want more."

The reaper's eyes glinted. "You do. Do you?"

Marcus was next to me in a flash. "Tessa? What are you doing?"

I raised a brow. "Something stupid. But I have to try," I told him. I exhaled and flicked my gaze back to the reaper as I said, "I want to be young again."

Malak laughed again. A crazy part of me wanted to flip him off, but that wouldn't go so well, so I kept my hands on my cane. "You made a deal with a demon to steal souls," said the reaper. "Did you really think there'd be no consequence? No payment? Especially as a *mortal* witch?"

My pulse hammered. "No, but I just didn't think it through. There wasn't time. I was right in the middle of saving souls when I made the deal to steal them." Yeah, that didn't come out right. "Do you have the power to make me young again?"

A smile of enjoyment blossomed over the reaper's face. "Yes," he said like it was a simple mundane request such as getting a haircut.

Okay then. Good. This was good. "How badly do you want your scythe? I can tell badly," I tried again, seeing some of the reaper's smile fade. "Listen. I'll get your scythe in exchange for Jack's wife, but I also want to be myself again. Young again. Can you do that? Jack's wife and my youth for your scythe? And me and my friends all walk out of here alive," I added, knowing that his quarrel with Marcus was still out on the table. "Deal?"

Malak leaned back into his couch. He puffed on his cigar and said, "Bring me my scythe and you have a deal."

23

Thank the cauldron I'd accepted Marcus's offer to drive us to Boston in his Jeep. I was so exhausted from traveling and stress. Then the use of that power word came back to bite me in the ass a half-hour later, which knocked me out cold. I'd slept all the way back home.

Though I'd slept like the dead, I had a few memories and glimpses of being in Marcus's strong arms, my head resting against his warm, hard chest, and of him putting me to bed. Too had I passed out again after that.

I dreamed of hundreds of Spanx coming at me, all lined up like chorus line dancers, trying to wrap me up tightly and suffocate me. Hildo was there. The cat peed on one of the Spanx and they faded. Don't ask. I couldn't control dreams.

I woke with a start and saw that I was still dressed. The Spanx was still wrapped tightly against my body, which was why I'd probably dreamed it was suffocating me. It really was.

"Iris! Help!" I yelled, not knowing if the Dark witch was in her room one floor below me, but it was worth a try.

The witch jumped into my room a moment later, landing in that karate kid crane kick pose. "What? What is it?"

I let out a sigh. "Spanx. The Spanx. Get it off! Get it off!"

I thought she was going to laugh, but only concern flashed on her face as she went to work. When she finally pulled off the Spanx, my pores and my lungs could breathe again.

"Thank the cauldron," I sighed, still lying on my bed. "It was suffocating me."

"Well, it's not meant to sleep in," she said, smiling this time. She moved to the hamper in the bathroom and dropped the Spanx in it.

I lifted my hand. "Help an old lady up. Would you? I need to wash the reaper's encounter off of me."

"Sure." Iris pulled me gently to my feet. "I'll start your shower. The hot water takes a while."

"What time is it?" I asked, looking for my phone on my dresser but not finding it there.

"It's half-past eight p.m.," called Iris, from the bathroom.

"Damn. I've been sleeping this whole time?"

Iris walked out. "You needed your rest. Don't give me those eyes. It's your body's way of telling you to stop. To slow down."

"It's my body's way of telling me to get used to that position. It'll be good practice for my coffin."

Iris rolled her eyes and I laughed. "Get in the shower, you old hag."

I lifted my chin. "That's exactly what I am. An old hag. And don't you forget it."

"I'll be downstairs if you need me." Iris disappeared out my bedroom door.

After a long shower, I pulled on a clean pair of sweatpants and hoodie (cause that's the only thing that fit) brushed my white and gray hair into a bun, and made my way downstairs to the kitchen.

I wasn't surprised to see Ronin—he loved a free meal—but I was startled to see Marcus sitting at the kitchen table having a beer. His attention flicked to me as I entered, and my stomach twisted in knots.

God, he looked good. The way the kitchen light cast shadows around the hard edges of his face made his gray eyes pop all sexy as hell. And me? Well, I didn't even try to put on any makeup. How could I? Everything would get lost in the folds of my skin.

Not to mention, I needed a magnifying glass to see what I was doing.

If things didn't go as planned tonight, this might be the last time I looked into those sexy gray eyes and that handsome face.

With the profound way he was staring at me, I could almost forget I was an eighty-year-old witch. But then I saw that second, barely noticeable sadness in his eyes... and it all came crashing down again.

"Are you hungry?" Ruth stood by the oven. "I've got some leftover veggie lasagna in the oven. It's still warm. Or, I could whip up anything you like."

I smiled at her and sat in the empty chair between Dolores and Beverly. "Not sure I can keep anything down. Maybe just some of your elixir of youth if you've got some?"

Ruth beamed. "Coming right up. I've got a new batch going right here," she said, grabbing a spoon and beginning to stir a steaming pot on the stove.

Dolores reached out and covered my hand with hers. "How are you feeling?"

"Spanx-less," I said happily, making Ronin spit out some of his beer. Yeah, I realized what that sounded like.

Beverly leaned back in her chair. "There's nothing wrong with a little spanking." She giggled. "When it's done right... it's quite enjoyable."

A loud crash of a plate dropping in the sink was followed by Iris looking up from the sink, her face red. "Sorry. Clumsy fingers."

Beverly cocked a brow. "See, Iris enjoys a little spanking too."

"Okay," I interjected. "Let's talk about something else." I saw a smile flash on Marcus's face, the kind that made heat coil in my belly and delicious tingles roll over my skin.

Dolores let go of my hand and leaned forward. She folded her hands on the kitchen table and frowned at them. "I'd like to talk about this trip to Egypt you're planning." She looked at me. "Marcus and Ronin filled us in," she offered, seeing the confusion on my face.

Here it comes...

Dolores slammed her hand on the table, making me jump. "How could you, Tessa? How could you make a deal with a reaper!" she howled. "Are you out of your mind?"

"Possibly. Skipping forward fifty years of life will do that to a person."

"She has a point," agreed Ronin, whose smile vanished just as Dolores flicked her scowl in his direction. He took a large gulp of his beer, staring at the tabletop like he was really into the polish.

"And you're going alone? Is that safe?" Ruth came

around and placed a steaming cup of that purple liquid on the table for me.

"It would take too long by plane," I answered and took a sip of the potion, feeling its effects of rejuvenation as soon as it hit my throat. "I don't know what to expect once I get to the pyramid. I'm not sure the people of Giza are going to let me wander around their sacred pyramids without permission. I have to be able to tap into a ley line and disappear if it comes to that. Hopefully, an old lady will go unnoticed." I flicked my gaze around my friends. "It's not that I don't want you guys to come. I just don't have much time left."

Iris grabbed the empty chair next to Ronin. "I hate it when you say that."

I flicked my gaze at the Dark witch. "It's the truth."

"So you're going to Egypt." Dolores watched me. "Do you even know how to get there?"

I tapped the bag on my lap. "I have my little black book of ley lines. There's a map of the world at the end of the book. It shows me which ley lines to take to get from here to Giza." I tried to keep the nerves from my voice. I'd never traveled that far before with a ley line. I'd never gone to another country, let alone another continent. The last time I jumped a ley line, it hadn't gone so well. Just calling up the ley lines had exhausted me.

But I'd slept enough. And with Ruth's elixir of youth regenerating my body somewhat, I might just make it. Then there was the trip back to think about.

"Ruth? You think you can give me some of your potion to go? To carry with me?"

Ruth's eyes widened in delight. "Of course. I'll fill up some vials for you. How many do you want? Three? Four?"

"I'll take four, thanks."

Beverly brushed a strand of hair back from her cheek. "You know, when I wear my black wig, everyone says I look just like Elizabeth Taylor in Cleopatra."

"Everyone as in your ego and its friends?" commented Dolores as a smile tweaked her lips.

Beverly arched a perfectly manicured brow at her sister. "You're just saying that because the only costume that suits you is Gandalf's."

I choked on my drink. "Hot," I said when Dolores's scowl came my way.

"I think this is foolish," said Dolores. "But I know you won't stay if I ask you to."

"I won't."

"And you're sure you can find this scythe?" inquired Dolores, giving me a look of pure calculation.

I shifted forward in my chair. "I know I can find it. Bringing it back... well, that's another story." I took a deep breath. "I have to try. If it'll mean I get my life back, I have to." I looked up at that moment to find Marcus staring at me, his jaw clenched and looking like he was about to beast out into his alter ego, King Kong.

"I don't like this one bit." Dolores's eyes flashed, and I could see a vein throbbing on her forehead. "You going all the way there. Alone. I just wish we could help in some way."

My gut twisted at the fear in her voice. I reached out and placed my hand on Dolores's. "You have. You've all helped me so much."

"Here you go." Ruth came over with four vials filled with purple liquid in her arms. She plopped them on the table, grabbed my bag, and began to fill it with them. "This should be enough for your trip back."

With the help of the table, I pulled myself up. "Thanks, Ruth."

My aunt beamed. "You're welcome."

I cast my gaze around the kitchen, looking at all those solemn faces and feeling as though my chest was caving in. "I should go." Because if I didn't go now, I might never leave.

"I'll walk you out." Marcus stood up just as Ronin and Iris pushed their chairs back and rose.

I looked at each of my aunts. "I'll see you later. Hopefully, as a thirty-year-old." When I saw that their eyes brimmed with tears, I spun around as quickly as I could before I started to sob.

Damn. I needed to get a hold on my emotions. I couldn't fall apart now. Not when I was so close.

I hobbled down the hallway, slipped my feet into my flats (I could not be bothered with boots now), and followed my friends outside into the cool night air.

When I reached the sidewalk where Ronin's BMW was parked, Iris turned around and hugged me. "You call me as soon as you get back," she said as she released me.

I nodded, finding it hard to speak. "I will."

I watched in silence as Ronin slipped behind the wheel, turned on the engine, and pulled out of the curb. Iris's worried face was plastered in the window of the passenger's seat.

"Is there a way I could convince you not to go?"

I turned around as Marcus took my free hand in his, the warmth and roughness of his skin on mine sending tiny thrills of delight stirring in my chest.

I shook my head, enjoying the heat coming off of him and finding myself leaning in before I could help myself.

"You okay?" he added, real concern in his voice. His eyes met mine, and my brow rose at the naked fear I saw in his eyes—fear for me.

A stir of emotions lifted through me. "Not really.

I think I'm a little bit crazy to do this, but at this point, crazy's all I've got."

Marcus peered at me, his thumb tracing a path on my hand. His touch brought back the memory of our time together with the sensations he was pulling from me.

His gray eyes were gentle. "I wish I could go with you," he said so softly I could barely hear him. Either that, or I was starting to lose my hearing.

"I know." I was glad he was here, and I pressed into him, soaking in his heat, the scent of something musky and male reaching me. He let go of my hand and wrapped his arms around me. I exhaled, letting my entire body blend into him and relaxing as I just took him in while I held him tightly. For a long moment, we stood there, holding each other, and part of me never wanted to let him go.

He pulled back a bit and I looked up at him. "What? Why are you looking at me like that?"

His smile widened, taking on a dash of pride. "It was great watching you with Malak. You're good at this."

I couldn't help my delighted grin. "I guess I am."

Marcus pulled me closer. "You know," he growled low. "They say the older the lady, the better the sex."

Heat from my core rushed to my face. "Stop," I

said, though the smile on my face said otherwise. "You're making this granny blush."

Marcus dipped his head and kissed me. It was soft and quick, his muscles tense and pressing against me. His hold on me was a shade too tight.

I felt the hint of tears prickle as I stared at him. My pulse jumped, not from lust but heartache. Marcus's grip on me tightened, and my throat closed in misery. He was going to be okay. He had to be.

Tears filled my eyes and I strained to keep them from falling. This was not the end.

My chest concaved at the unspoken words between us. "I'll be fine."

"I know," he answered, but I could tell he didn't believe it. Though I knew he had faith in me and my abilities, I could tell he was terrified of being helpless. He couldn't be there for me. He couldn't protect me, and that was killing him.

Almost in tears, I blinked fast, my throat burning. "I'll be back before you know it."

His gray eyes turned intense and heavy. "You better be."

I pulled away before I started bawling and pressed my hand to his chest. "Go. Go before I change my mind." I could feel my resolve fading.

"Hurry back," he pleaded. The chief watched me for a beat longer and his arms fell away from me reluctantly. With a final look, he walked away.

Leaning heavily on Gran's cane, I watched him get behind the wheel of his Jeep and drive away until he turned left at the end of Stardust Drive and was gone.

"Finally. I thought he'd never leave."

I jerked at the voice behind me. Frowning, I turned around. "Jack? What the hell are you doing here?"

The soul collector stepped from behind the tall spruce. Briefcase in tow and wearing his signature dark suit and fedora, the light from the streetlamp shone on his pale skin making it almost appear to be glowing.

The snow crunched under his shoes at his approach. "Did you see my Carrie? How did she look? Did he hurt her? Did you tell her I miss her? That I'm trying to get her back? That I love her?"

I felt a tug on my chest at the worry in the demon's tone. "She looked okay. She's fine. She's alive." I thought it best to leave out the chain part.

Jack smiled and that made me feel worse. The truth was, Carrie, didn't look so hot. She didn't have much time left. Neither did I. We were both expiring, so I had to move quickly.

I stared at the demon, a frown lowering my brow. "You still haven't answered my question. What are you doing here? If you came here to back down from our deal... I think I might just strangle you."

Jack shook his head. "No. No. No. Our deal remains."

"Good. I have to go," I told the soul collector. "I don't have much time." I'd said it for me, but it was also true about his wife.

"Did it work? Did you make a trade for my wife's life?"

"I did."

At that, Jack looked visibly less stressed out. "What did he ask for?"

I thought about it a moment, wondering if I should trust him with that information. "His scythe. Apparently, it was taken from him and placed somewhere, loaded with wards and protection spells." Obviously, someone didn't want him to get it back, but I didn't have time to think about the reasons right now.

Jack adjusted his hat. "I'm coming with you."

My lips parted. "No, you're not."

"Yes, I am." Jack's face wrinkled, and the lines of his face deepened as though a lifetime of pain had fallen on him at that moment. "She's my wife. I can't let you do this alone. You're going to need me."

I thought about it a moment. The reaper hadn't said I couldn't ask for help. And Jack could world-jump just about anywhere he wanted, and just as fast as the ley lines.

"Fine."

"Yes?" He looked surprised. "Yes. Good. That's good. Um. Where are we going?"

I floundered in my bag, grabbed one of the vials Ruth had made for me, removed the cork stopper, and took a swig. I swallowed and said, "To the pyramid of Menkaure."

"Interesting. Did he say who put it there?"

"No." I shook my head. "Meet me inside. And watch yourself. It's probably going to be daylight out." Not waiting for an answer, I pulled on the ley lines nearest me and felt their power thrum through my body.

"Let's get your Carrie back," I said and jumped.

24

Traveling to another continent at the speed of light in the body of an eighty-year-old woman in a ley line was not my cup of tea. It wasn't my cup of anything, really, since I had to constantly try to control the contents of my stomach so Ruth's potion wouldn't spew out of my mouth.

Her rejuvenating drink was the only thing that kept me standing and strong enough to hold the ley lines while I counted the stops.

And there were many, many ley line stops.

Each stop was like going up the roller coaster ride—and then down in one second. My stomach rolled and bounced, lodging somewhere in my throat and then settling back down again. Energy rushed through my head, my body, everywhere.

Riding a ley line across an ocean was like riding

my own private jet. If I'd been in my thirty-year-old body, I would have probably been screaming my head off in delight and excitement. As it was, I was screaming my head off in dread and sudden jolts of pain in my knees, hips, and ankles.

I was surprised I was still standing. I probably would have been more comfortable sitting on my butt, but I was a stubborn and proud old witch. Yeah, I said it. Old witch. Because that's exactly what I was.

Thousands of ley lines were placed at strategic points around the world. You just had to pick the nearest ley line to your destination—which, in this case, was the one in Giza going straight through the pyramid of Menkaure—and hop on.

I'd half expected to see my father, but he didn't show.

After about thirty minutes, I approached the fiftieth stop. If I missed my stop, I was screwed. Just riding the ley line was stripping me of most of my energy. I didn't have the luxury of jumping in and out of ley lines if I missed my stop.

And just like all the other stops, the propulsion around me slowed. The images around me focused, and I could see endless rolls of golden dunes and blue skies. I heard no sounds except the rushing of wind in my ears.

Three large triangular shapes came into view—the pyramids of Giza. Nestled around them were three smaller triangular structures. I felt like I was watching a National Geographic special on the pyramids of Egypt with a front-row seat. It was great.

I made for the smallest of the three pyramids, the pyramid of Menkaure. The ley line took me straight through and inside the pyramid. When the sunlight was cut off and I was surrounded in darkness, I hauled myself out.

And hit a wall.

I fell to the ground on something soft. If it weren't for that soft landing, I would have probably broken a knee, a hip, or even a wrist.

"Not so bad. Could have been worse." I blinked into the darkness and was assaulted by the strong smell of mold, urine, and something else unholy.

"Okay. Gross. If I'm sitting in a pile of mummy poo, I'm going to kill someone."

While on the ground and still in darkness, I shoved my hand in my bag, felt a cool, smooth ball the size of an apple, and yanked out a witch orb supplied by my aunt Dolores.

I tossed it in the air and said, "Da mihi lux." *Give me light.*

Bright yellow light spilled from a hovering globe, illuminating the space and casting enough light for me to see the rough limestone walls.

Turned out I was not sitting in mummy poo but rather a pile of old discarded clothes. Still gross. I pulled myself up with Gran's cane and looked around.

I was in some sort of chamber with a curved ceiling made of the same limestone. Five cut-out doorways faced me. Moving toward them, the witch orb following me, I inspected each one carefully. Taking my time, I moved my fingers over the limestone in search of secret levers or just a pulse of magic. There was nothing here. No magical wards that I could sense. Nothing. Just more empty nooks, dust, and sand.

It occurred to me that if Malak's scythe had been hidden in here for centuries, it was more likely that thieves or archeologists might have taken it. Maybe it was gone. Maybe it wasn't even here.

I sighed and shuffled to the middle of the chamber. My head pounded, and I started to sweat. I could feel the exhaustion, my body's way of telling me to stop, but I couldn't.

I yanked out another one of Ruth's vials and downed it in one giant gulp. Immediately, I could feel some of the exhaustion lifting, the strength in my legs and body returning.

"Jack?" I called as low as I could, not wanting to alert any guards if any were posted outside. Where the hell was that soul collector?

"I'm in the tomb chamber," came his voice.

I turned to the sound and saw a set of steps that

led off to another chamber. Wiping my mouth with the back of my hand, I dropped the empty vial back in my bag and climbed the steps.

"How long have you been here?" I grumbled, angry that he hadn't told me he was here. I pulled myself up from the last step and entered another chamber, smaller than the other one with a lower ceiling.

Just as my foot hit the stone floor, I was hit with the overwhelming thrum of power, of magic. Some serious wards were in here. We were definitely in the right place.

I let out my senses to get a feel of this magic. The power of the patchwork of wards hummed steadily, like a gazillion volts of electricity in the air.

"I got here ten minutes ago." The soul collector stood facing a wall, staring at it with one hand clasped around his chin like he could see something of great interest there. "This doesn't make any sense."

"What doesn't?" Curious, I squinted in the semi-darkness. I couldn't see a thing. As I moved next to him, my witch orb followed and illuminated the wall.

My mouth fell open.

The wall was an array of images, hieroglyphics, and symbols. I was surprised at how well-preserved they were like they'd been freshly painted a few days ago. My eyes rolled around the magnificent images of men and women painted in profile, worshiping their gods with some sitting in boats. I saw images of birds and cats, drawings of eyes, and a multitude of symbols along the edges like a frame. It was beautiful and mesmerizing.

And when my gaze moved to a spot on the far right, my pulse quickened.

I saw an image of a large, dark man with a shaved head. And in his hand was an Egyptian sickle.

A scythe. The reaper's scythe.

"That's it." My heart thrummed excitedly. "Very clever hiding it with the hieroglyphics."

"Yes," agreed the soul collector. "Clever indeed. So... how do you suppose we take it?"

I turned my eyes back on the wall. "Right. How *do* we take it? It won't be that simple if the reaper can't and his magic workers couldn't." The continuous hum of the wards pulsed against my face, the air crackling with power. Damn. What did I get myself into?

Jack turned and faced me. "Sometimes the easiest strategy is the right one."

"Meaning?"

"Perhaps you should just... *take it* and see what happens."

I scowled at the soul collector. "I should just *take it*. And get my own ass fried? No thanks."

"Well, better yours than mine," offered the demon.

"How thoughtful."

"You're welcome." Jack made a sound in his throat, something between the sound of an inkling and annoyance. "I've discovered two things while you took your time getting here."

I clenched my jaw. "I didn't take my time, Captain Jack. I came here as fast as I could." I leaned on my cane so I wouldn't be tempted to smack him with it. "What have you discovered?"

Jack turned his white eyes back on the wall. "One, this is some sort of celestial magic. And two, being a demon, touching it would most definitely kill me. This magic is the opposite of mine."

"Celestial magic?" The reaper being an angel, that made sense. But I was still confused. What the hell was celestial magic?

The demon nodded. "Yes. If I touch this wall," he gestured with his hands, "poof. I will cease to exist." He laughed, though it sounded forced.

I cocked a brow. "Does that mean my contract would be null?" I offered, a smile on my face.

Jack was shaking his hand. "It *must* be you. You have to do it."

"It must be me," I repeated, trying to find the

answer to this riddle but feeling like my brain was full of cotton balls. I sighed, pulling my eyes back on the painting of the man with the scythe. "It's an image painted on the wall. An image of the scythe. So, how do I make it come alive? I have to touch it. Right? Mutter a few spells and voila. How else could this work?" I knew it wouldn't be so easy.

"Give it a try," encouraged the demon. "You're a witch. A witch cast these wards. It makes logical sense that only a witch can retrieve it. Do your witch."

"Do my witch?"

"Do your magic. Call your inner witch."

"But you said this was celestial magic."

"That a witch cast." Jack's white eyes settled on me. "You're different. A witch with a demon father. A witch who travels on ley lines. You're the one," he said as he stepped back from the wall to give me the room to work. "You're the one who can get my Carrie back."

Right. No pressure. The idea of that poor female demon at the mercy of that reaper had Ruth's tonic rising in my throat.

"Fine. I'll do my witch."

Exhaling, I shambled a little closer to the image of the man holding the sickle or the scythe, my heart hammering away in my ears. Maybe Jack was right. Maybe I was the only one who could retrieve it.

Holding on to that thought, I tapped into the elements around me, reached out my knobby hand hovering an inch from the wall, and placed my palm on the scythe.

Spectral, white-blue light flared up around me. So far so good. Next came a surge of power. Not like the hot, unpleasant pricks of magic. It was more like plunging down a slide made of sandpaper naked, and it hurt like hell. I screamed as energy seared through my blood and every cell of my body in a way that would have been damaging to a mortal person, maybe even fatal.

Then I got the blast.

Something hit me in the chest, and I flew back until I hit the wall, which took exactly one second. I slid down in a pile of old lady bones, a cane, and dirty sweats.

"Guess you're not the one," said Jack, staring down at me as disappointment flashed across his pale face.

I unclenched my jaw. "I hate you."

25

After an hour of testing every spell and power word I could remember, I was sweating and exhausted and no closer to figuring out this celestial magic. My temper was darkening by the second.

"What the hell is celestial magic anyway?" I yelled and threw a loose stone at the wall. Nothing happened.

Jack shrugged. "The magic of creation. Of the heavens. Magic of the stars, of the universe. Blah-blah-blah."

"Nice." Leaning with my back on the wall opposite the one with the hieroglyphics, I sat on the cold ground with *The Witch's Handbook, Volume Three* on my lap. I flipped through the pages. "I've been through it ten times. There's nothing here on celestial magic or how to make something flat solid again. Or how to make something come alive again."

"Try harder."

I glowered at the demon and pointed my cane in his direction, below the belt. "You know what else canes are good for?"

Jack cupped his hands over his groin. "You've got a dirty mind."

"I'm tired. Old, no thanks to you, and hungry. We're stuck in the middle of the desert inside a pyramid that smells like pee. So forgive me for being a little temperamental."

The soul demon did something that surprised me. He came over and sat down next to me. He took off his hat and said, "If they were able to place the scythe inside this wall, there must be a way to pull it out again."

"Who's they?"

His bald head gleamed in the light of the witch orb. "The legion of angels. I heard the stories. Not sure if they're all true, but the legion took away the reaper's scythe because he was killing humans with it. The scythe severs the link between the body and the soul. The soul is then absorbed into the scythe. It gives the bearer of the weapon tremendous power."

My shoulders slumped. "Fantastic. And here we are trying to give it back. I knew it had to be something bad. Why else would they make it so he couldn't get his hands on it again."

"Make no mistake, Tessa. I don't care about a few measly humans. I care only about my wife."

"I figured as much. I would have been really surprised if you did care about some poor humans since you trick them into giving up their souls."

"I don't trick them... I simply... show them a different way."

I raised a brow. "You tricked me."

Jack pursed his lips. "I did," he agreed like it was no big deal having tricked me into working for him for the rest of my life.

I shook my head, not wanting and too tired to have this conversation. "But he's an angel? How can he do that?"

"He's a reaper," answered the demon, as though that were answer enough.

"He promised to make me young again, you know," I told the demon after a long moment of silence, not knowing why I was sharing or comfortable sharing because I realized that I was. Weird. "I get him his scythe, you get Carrie, and I get my youth."

Jack pulled his hat over his head. "It's a good deal. Two for one. You are good at this. A real natural. Maybe you should rethink our deal."

"No."

Jack laughed. I didn't think I'd ever heard him genuinely laugh before. Again weird.

I looked at the soul collector demon and flashed him a smile. "Hey. Are we bonding?"

Jack snorted, looking slightly uncomfortable. "Of course not."

My smile grew. "Are we friends?"

"We are much better than friends. We are allies."

I laughed. "God, I must be really tired because you're making so much sense."

Feeling slightly put out, I rested my head on the wall. I hurt everywhere. Not as much as when the ward attacked me but close. My legs, hips, and knees creaked and ached. So did my lower back, like I'd been kicked several times.

I glanced inside my bag. I had one more vial of Ruth's tonic left. I couldn't take it now. I needed it for when I returned to the club with the reaper's scythe. *If* I returned with it. And at the rate things were going, that was a big if.

I'd exhausted every possible spell I could think of. Even Jack was at a loss.

We were screwed, and my gut tightened at the thought of Carrie.

Jack jumped to his feet, making me jerk, and began pacing the small chamber.

"What?" I cried out. "Why are you so fidgety all of a sudden. You're freaking me out,"

Jack spun around, his eyes round. "Because in about five minutes, the guards are going to let in the tourists. That's why."

Oh, crap.

"Why did it have to be celestial magic," growled the demon, holding on to his hat as though just uttering the words would cause his hat to fly off his head. I could see he was losing it. "Witch magic would have been a breeze. Demon magic, piece of cake. But n-o-o-o-o it has to be celestial. Always celestial with these damn angels."

"Maybe it's because they're *angels*," I drawled.

And then I had another lightbulb moment.

"This *is* celestial magic," I repeated, my pulse increasing, feeling like I was onto something. "And being a demon, it would kill you."

"Yes. What of it?" said Jack annoyed, bringing his attention back to me.

I furrowed my brow in thought. "And you said this magic was the *opposite* of you."

"Yes. Yes. So what? If we don't get our hands on that scythe, what difference does it make?"

"It would explain why the other mages and witches couldn't retrieve it. All I need to do is cancel out the wards." I blinked up at him. "That's it. I've figured it out," I beamed.

"What?" Jack hissed at me. "You're not making sense."

I threw up my hand. "Help me up." Jack took hold of my hand, and it didn't even bother me to feel his touch, cold and dry, as he hauled me to my feet.

"Why are you smiling?" Jack's already-pale face paled even more as he handed me my cane. "We've got minutes. *Minutes* before the human troops arrive, and all will be lost. I'm going to lose my wife!"

"You won't, but I'm going to need your blood."

"You need my blood?" repeated the demon, looking at me like I'd lost my mind.

I shifted my weight around with the help of the cane. "Yes. It's perfect. I need your demon blood. I have some, but it probably won't be enough. Your blood and my power word should be enough."

"To destroy the wards?" questioned the demon as he looked at the wall of hieroglyphics.

"Exactly," I answered, my adrenaline flowing. "Your blood to counter the celestial magic, and then I can carry the scythe since you probably can't touch it."

"No," Jack shook his head. "No, I cannot."

My head hurt, and my heart was pounding so hard. It was going to work. I knew it was.

I shambled across the chamber until I was facing the image of the dark man and the scythe. "Cough up some blood, demon," I ordered.

Jack was staring at me still as though a third arm

had just sprouted from my forehead, but the demon did as he was told.

He pulled out a small knife from inside his jacket and sliced it across his palm. Black blood oozed from his cut.

"Hurry," I urged, hearing two distinct voices coming from somewhere above us. "Throw some on the wall."

Jack did as I instructed and flicked his wounded hand at the wall, sending a spray of black blood over the hieroglyphs.

The effect was instantaneous.

The wards flared up again, sending a spectral of white-blue light around us, but they were cut off. Steam rose from where the demon's blood hit the wall, and the smell of sulfur and rot rose around us.

I drew in a breath and lifted my chin. Feeling more confident, and with a smile, I pulled on the elements around me and cried, "Accendo!"

Energy rushed out of me as a ball of fire thrust out of my outstretched hand and slammed into the wall of limestone.

The chamber exploded in a blast of kinetic energy and wind. Dust and chunks of rock flew everywhere as the wall of hieroglyphs cracked and collapsed.

Whoops.

And then a heavy, four-foot-long metal sickle fell to the stone floor with an echoing crash.

The reaper's scythe.

"You did it!" exclaimed the soul collector, and I beamed at the admiration in his voice.

Speaking of voices, I could hear shouts coming from above and the sound of people running down the stairs.

"We've gotta go." I lowered myself carefully and clasped my hand around the scythe. I flinched, nearly dropping it.

A darkness, an icy pull of death that nearly suffocated me thrummed through my body until it faded and became bearable again. The whisper of voices sounded in my head. What the hell was that?

"What is it?" asked Jack. "Does it burn? Oh, no, you can't touch it!"

"That's not it." I stared at the scythe, a sick feeling washing over me. "I can feel something. I think it's souls." But as I stared at the weapon, all I saw was gleaming silver metal carved with intricate designs and spidery symbols that I'd never seen before.

"It's fine," I told the worried demon, just as the screeching of a gate being pulled across a stone floor reached me. "Meet me outside the reaper's club," I instructed, my pulse racing.

Jack smiled. "Got it." His eyes widened, and for a

moment they looked wet. I felt some joy for him. "Thank you," he added, surprising me.

And with a pop of displaced air, the soul collector vanished.

Yeah, we were definitely friends... or becoming friends.

Smiling, I pulled on the ley line and jumped.

26

By the time I got back to Boston, it was around midnight.

The streets were quieter than usual for a Friday night as darkness rushed in, filling the spaces not lit by the streetlights. Cars and cabs honked at a distance as I crossed the street, wet with snow, and headed for the reaper's club, GRIM.

I was tired, and the scythe slipped in my grip, but I held on. The weight of it, the darkness, was weighing me down and draining me. I couldn't wait to give it to the reaper.

I was wire tight, exhausted from traveling and the use of my magic, tension pulling me in every direction. Once I crossed the street, I took a moment, balancing the scythe on my hip, and gulped the last of the elixir of youth so I wouldn't collapse like an idiot.

Because someone was watching me. The same someone that I'd blasted through the door the first time I was here.

Once I felt the strength in my legs returning, I shambled forward again. My shoes slipped on the wet snow as I approached the bouncer, doorwere, doordog, whatever.

The massive man eyed me like I was an annoying mosquito buzzing around his head that he wanted to swat. I didn't blame him after what I'd done.

But if he was going to give me a hard time again, I was going to have to blast his ass again.

I cast my gaze around the street and the line of buildings. Jack wasn't here. Nervousness started to tickle up my spine. I was beginning to think of Jack as my backup. I'd expected him to come in with me to face Malak as a team. The soul collector should have been here by now. Where was he? Had something happened to him? He wouldn't miss the chance of getting his wife back.

I couldn't wait. Now I'd have to face the big reaper on my own. Swell.

Hunched over, I stood in front of the bouncer and said, "Looks like you've got a new door?" He didn't even blink. "Right. Well. I have something for Malak."

The bouncer stepped aside and opened the door for me. He never took his eyes off of me as he held the door open and waited.

"Thanks," I said. Might as well be polite.

With the scythe in my left hand and my cane in my right, I made my way carefully through the entrance as that sad, dark classical music blasted around me. I passed the bar and crossed the dance floor, careful not to bump into the few paranormals who were dancing. If you wanted to call it dancing. More like sleepwalking with sudden abrupt arm movements like they suffered from spasms.

I made for the same door where Marcus took us the first time I was here and did just as he did.

I knocked twice.

The door swung open and the same pretty woman with short red hair and covered in tattoos stood in the threshold. Her eyes flicked to the scythe in my hands and then she too stepped aside to let me in.

All right then.

I shuffled across the game room until I stood in almost the exact spot I had previously. Ignoring the group of paranormals whose attention all snapped to me as soon as I walked through the door, my eyes tracked the room until they landed on the petite, sickly female lying on the floor, her necklace of iron chains still wrapped around her. With her cheeks sunken, she looked like she hadn't eaten in a month. She looked worse than before, but at least she was still alive.

"I can't believe you did it."

I looked up just as the powerfully built frame of the angel crossed the room. His ebony skin was a stark contrast to the white shirt he wore.

I opened my mouth, and he yanked the scythe out of my grip, nearly throwing me to the ground in the process. Thankfully, Gran's cane kept me upright.

Yeah, really hated this guy.

Malak's gaze lit as he admired the scythe. He held the heavy weapon easily in his thick hand, twisting it skillfully like he was testing it and remembering the feel of it.

Malak laughed. "You fucking did it." When he finally looked at me, he said, "I underestimated you."

"I get that a lot."

The reaper watched me with a curious expression. "Curious, how you, an old, withered witch, with a frail, broken body, beat the world's most powerful mages and sorcerers."

"That's me." I looked around the room, noticing how everyone was smiling and not in a good way. They gave me the creeps, and I felt a cold chill snake up my spine up to my hairline.

I moved my gaze back to Carrie. She was

watching me from her spot on the floor, her eyes round with a desperate hope that tore at my heart.

Hang on, I told her with my eyes, hoping she'd get the message.

In a blur, Malak spun on the spot and brought the scythe down in a skillful arc, cutting the air around him.

Wisps of my hair flew back from my face. That was close. I took a step back.

"Yes," he said lovingly, twisting his scythe in his grasp while gazing at it like a loving pet, as though it were alive. Maybe it was. "How I missed you, my darling."

Okay. That was my cue to go.

"So, about our deal," I said, my voice harsh, carrying the pains and exhaustion of my night. Again my eyes fell on the crowd of paranormals, and again they kept giving me their creepy smiles like they knew something I didn't.

"You can take the demon whore with you," said Malak. "I've no more use for her." He took a step in her direction. With a powerful thrust, he brought the scythe down hard. It hit part of the iron chain that was hooked to a ring on the floor. The chain began to glow red and then it crumbled to ash.

Okay, so the scythe wasn't just to sever mortal souls. Good to know.

Carrie's eyes widened with both fear and hope as she pushed herself up on shaky legs and hurried over to me. I cringed at her thin frame.

"Thank you," she said, her voice barely audible as she nearly collapsed into my arms. Her time was running out.

"You're going to be fine," I told her, straining as I steadied myself from her sudden weight as it pulled me down. "You'll be with Jack soon."

Carrie flashed me the tiniest of smiles, twitchy, as though her face had forgotten the emotion.

With her added weight, my knees wobbled under the strain. If I didn't get my thirty-year-old legs back soon, I doubted we'd make it out the door of the club.

I looked back at the reaper. "Okay. I'm ready."

Malak stopped twirling his scythe and turned very slowly in my direction. He cocked an eyebrow at me and said, "I like older women, but I don't do fossils." At that, his paranormal cronies all threw back their heads and laughed like a bunch of wild hyenas.

"Wait? What?" I decided not to point out that he was a gazillion years older than me. Carrie was sliding down my side, so I hauled her up as best as I could. "No. I mean. I'm ready for you to make me young again."

The reaper turned from me and made his way back to his couch. He sat and placed the scythe on the empty spot next to him, never taking his hand off of it.

He gave me a cold smile. "I'm not making you young again."

The redhead on his left giggled, and I wanted to kick her in the mouth.

A spark of hatred flashed through me. "We had a deal. I get you your scythe and I get Carrie and my youth."

"I changed it."

The world around me wavered as I drew in breath after breath. This had been my only shot. And I'd been played.

"You bastard," I seethed as angry tears welled in my eyes, my balance shaky.

Malak took a deep breath, scenting me and relishing in my pain, my despair. "Careful now. Or you'll leave with nothing."

Carrie whimpered. My stomach clenched at her fear and panic. Yes, he'd screwed me, but I wasn't about to let her die. My deal with Jack was still good. I was going to be an eighty-year-old woman, but I'd still have a life.

The tears started the dribble out, one by one. I felt numb, betrayed, and the winning emotion was feeling like a fool. I wanted to curse this sonovabitch.

I wanted to blast his ass back to the heavens. I wanted to use the scythe and cut off his heavenly jewels.

Instinctively, I pulled on the elements around me, almost panting and seeing the laughing faces around me. The reaper's eyes narrowed in greed and anger. The power of the elements hummed through me, wanting to be let go.

And I wanted to oblige.

The reaper's expression changed to mocking, his dark eyes spiteful. "I'm not sure I like the way you're looking at me." He laughed. "Because it looks like you want to *hurt* me. Do you want to hurt me, witch?"

I clenched my jaw and glared at him.

Malak's cold, uncaring smile was like a slap in the face. "I'll tell you what." He leaned forward. "Run, before I change my mind, witch."

He didn't need to tell me twice.

Holding on to Carrie, I spun us around as fast as my eighty-year-old legs could muster, and we wobbled out the room like a pair of drunks.

A lump filled my throat as grief and betrayal slammed into me. I staggered forward, as Carrie and I both supported one another across the dance floor.

Wavering on our feet, we stumbled out the club's main entrance and out the door into the night air.

Panting, we teetered for a moment, two desperate souls, lost.

Movement caught my eye. Jack was rushing toward us. I nearly sobbed at the sight of him.

The soul collector swooped in, wrapped us both into his arms, and downtown Boston disappeared.

27

When life threw me a curveball, I got hit in the face.

So my plans had taken a bit of a nosedive down the shitter. When I thought about it, this was the worst outcome I'd ever found myself in. It was sort of depressing to imagine my life as the few years I had left and not all the years I had in front of me.

But I didn't always get what I wished for, and life had a way of making that happen.

I sat on the floor, next to a golden retriever with her tongue lolling practically to the floor. Nearby, a German shepherd with a green and red parrot perched on his shoulder, three toads, two snakes, and three ravens kept their distance from the three cats huddled together near my feet.

I was just too exhausted and angry to stand,

staring up at that strange, metal contraption that held all of Jack's collected souls. Hildo's purring was my only comfort at this point, and knowing that we were about to be free almost made me smile.

The black cat looked up at me from my lap, yellow eyes glistening with sorrow. "I'm sorry you can't get your 'lives' back."

"Me too," I said, stroking his head and watching his eyes close in relaxation.

"So, Malak was a dick," said the cat, his eyes open again.

"A huge dick." Wow. That didn't come out right.

"I could have told you that. Can't say I'm surprised." The cat flicked his ears around his head. "But you did manage to save the soul collector's wife. That's something."

I smiled down at the cat, rubbing my fingers through his silky black fur. "And your soul. All your souls," I said, looking at the familiars. Knowing that I had saved their souls did bring me some joy. It hadn't all been for nothing.

Hildo pinned me with his yellow eyes. "What will you do with your free time? Now that you're not stuck on duty with this pale bastard."

I sighed. "I don't know. For starters, I think I'll get myself a nice rocking chair."

The cat turned away and started to lick one of his

front paws. "You know, I'm an expert at keeping old ladies company."

"What?" I laughed.

"Well, if you want," continued the cat, setting his paw down with his eyes back on mine, "once my soul is free... you could bring me back. I could live with you. Be your familiar, witch companion."

My lips parted in a silent "o." "You're kidding. That could work? For real?"

"Oh, sure. It's a simple spell. You've got the witch chomps like I've never seen before. It'll be a breeze for you. Your aunts have it written somewhere. I mean, the afterlife is great and all, but I've got so much more living to do. I'm not ready to rest just yet."

My chest swelled with emotion so fast that I had to fight down a sob. "Okay then. If you want. Yeah. I think that would be really nice. We kinda make a good team." I thought I might transition to my new life with a lot less heartache with Hildo by my side.

"Done." Hildo blinked up at me and added, "Oh, and just FYI. I only eat fresh food. No dried kibble. I'm a familiar. Not a house cat. And the only thing I'll eat from a can is tuna, sardines, and caviar. In water. Not the gross oil stuff. It's a disaster trying to get it out of my whiskers."

"Look at you," I laughed, "already with the demands." I was really starting to like this cat. I had a feeling my aunts would love him too, especially Ruth.

I heard footsteps approaching, and I turned around toward the sound.

Jack and Carrie were coming our way. Carrie smiled at me when our eyes met, her hands clasped behind her back like she was hiding something. She looked good, healthy. As soon as we'd touched down in the in-between, her transformation began. It was like looking at a bent, drooping flower in desperate need of water. And as soon she got her water, in this case, a dose of her world, Carrie blossomed into a healthy-looking, though very petite, female demon.

She was very charming and kind. She'd dropped the horrid glitter bikini and opted for a long, flowing dark skirt, white linen top, and short denim jacket. She gave off a more bohemian chic vibe. I liked it.

While we'd waited for Jack to get my original contract, which surprised me since I thought he'd carried it with him always, we started talking.

Apparently, she was a tikoloshe demon and the true ancestors of the faeries. She was skilled at growing things and had a shop of flowers and sold exotic fruits somewhere in the city, she'd told me. A city in the Netherworld. It was hard to wrap my head around that.

"I'll go see what's keeping him," she'd told me

about ten minutes ago. Then she'd disappeared into the darkness.

I truly didn't understand how the demons could maneuver in this place. It was like an abyss. To me, there was only darkness. But maybe to them, it was entirely different.

"Ah. Tessa. Here you are," said Jack, as though he was surprised to see me.

"Where else would I be?" I asked as Hildo jumped off my lap and settled on the floor next to me. Like I was going to leave without seeing my contract destroyed? I didn't think so.

"As promised, I have your contract." Jack produced a scroll of parchment from inside his jacket. My contract. The one I forgot to read thoroughly before signing, the damn piece of paper that started this mess.

"Can I see it?" I asked.

Jack nodded. "Of course."

"Let me help you up," said Carrie, who for someone petite pulled me to my feet with a surprising amount of ease. She handed me my cane.

"Thanks," I said as I leaned on it, glad for the support.

Jack stepped closer and handed me the contract. I took it, unfurled the paper, and brought it close to my face. I recognized the wording and my signature at the bottom. Yup. This was the contract that sealed my fate to the soul collector.

I looked up from the paper. "So, how does this work? Do we sign an amendment?"

Jack and Carrie shared a look. Then Jack raised his hand and snapped his fingers.

With a small pop of yellow and red flames, the contract in my hands dissolved into a cloud of ash.

"There you have it," announced Jack. "Contract dissolved," he added with a smile.

I stared at the ashes at my feet, feeling numb and not as happy as I thought I'd be or should feel. "And them?" I looked at the animals around me. "Their souls are freed, right?" If he turned on me now, I was going to clobber him with my cane.

"Absolutely." Jack clapped his hands once, and then a light, a glowing white light emanated from each animal as though a lightbulb had been switched on inside each of them.

I stared, fascinated as each animal, in turn, became a bright light until I couldn't see the animal anymore, just a bright, fractal, pulsing white light.

I squinted in the bright light, searching for the black cat. "Hildo?"

"See you on the other side," came Hildo's voice, though all I could see was a brilliant white light where the cat had been a moment ago.

I blinked, and the lights were gone. All of them. The familiars had vanished.

The tightness in my chest lessened a bit at seeing the familiar souls freed and that Jack had kept his promise. Strange that an angel wouldn't keep his promise, but a demon would. Perhaps it wasn't that strange after all.

"Well," I sighed, pulling my gaze back at the demon couple. "Guess that's my cue to leave."

Carrie frowned at her husband and elbowed him in the side. She raised her brows suggestively like he was forgetting something.

"Oh! I almost forgot." Jack's white eyes were round, and he had a strange smile on his face.

"Forgot what?" I eyed them suspiciously. "What are you two planning? I can see your brains working."

Carrie had her lips clamped tightly, trying not to smile, but it wasn't working. Yeah, something was definitely up with them.

Jack walked up to his soul containment machine, turned back at me, and said, "There's one more thing I need to do before you leave."

"Yeah. What's that?" I leaned on my cane, trying to see what he was doing.

"This." From the folds of his jacket, the soul collector pulled out a rusty metal skeleton key, with a large, oval bow and long shaft.

With a flick from his wrist, he inserted it in a keyhole on the machine I hadn't noticed was there before and turned it. After a click, he pressed the green button and pulled down the lever.

The machine gave a rattle and started humming. A compartment opened, and Jack stood back as a string of glowing white spheres shot out from the slot. They spun in the air, circling above us like brilliant stars in a night sky.

And then they raced directly at me.

Pulse fast, my knees buckled but I stayed upright. Like a vortex, they spun around me, a whirlpool of light. And then the souls went *inside* me.

I gasped as I felt a lightning path straight to my core. I arched my back as the souls entered my body, filling me with light and filling my essence with a bright, warm glow of power, letting it leak into my soul. The power of souls.

It was like bathing in light. It was amazing.

I felt a release as the light diminished until the souls disappeared.

I looked up to the two smiling faces of Jack and Carrie. "What just happened? Where did the souls go?" I asked, a little shaken.

Jack shrugged and said, "Heaven. The afterlife. I've released them. They're free to go where they want."

Carrie stepped up to me and handed me a small pink hand mirror. "Here. Take a look."

With trembling fingers, I took the mirror. And then with a deep breath, I lifted it up and looked at myself.

And swore.

And swore some more.

"My father was right," I exclaimed, staring at my smooth, wrinkle-free face. I touched it with my hand, just in case, this was some sort of glamour. Nope. All real. I blinked and smiled at the face staring back at me, the face I recognized but thought I'd never see again except in pictures.

"Your father?" asked Jack with a puzzled expression.

"Nothing," I said giving Carrie back her mirror and blinking fast. I didn't want to get my father into trouble with the soul collector. I didn't want anything to ruin this moment. I smiled, starting to feel the overwhelming emotions and fear from the last month starting to dissolve.

I'd been ready to live as an eighty-year-old woman. I wasn't thrilled about it, having missed those years in between, but I had accepted it. I'd accepted the consequences of my actions and taken the responsibilities for my mistakes. But this was better.

I looked at Jack and his wife, and I felt a kind of

kinship forming in my gut, something new. Guess we were friends after all.

Jack's eyes were on me, a pleased smile on his face that said he'd saved the day, though he'd been the one to put me in this position in the first place. But I wasn't about to bring it up.

But the real kicker was the thought of Marcus's face when he saw me. It also gave me some R-rated thoughts. What? He owed me a birthday dinner in his lovely, lovely birthday suit.

"I should go," I told them, smiling. I wasn't sure if I'd ever see them again, but a little voice inside me said that I would.

"Good luck, Tessa," said Carrie. "And thank you."

I wasn't sure what to say to that, so I just smiled.

"My work is done here," said Jack. "So long, Tessa Davenport."

The last thing I saw was Jack's arm wrapped around his wife's waist, a wide grin spread over his face, and then my world faded to black.

28

I woke to two yellow eyes staring at me.

My heart pounded, sending bits of adrenaline through my body. After a few beats, the comfortable sleeping haze shredded, the fading of dreamland, and I pulled myself fully awake. I wasn't dreaming. A cat sat on my chest, the weight of him making him very real, and obstructing my breathing.

"You're heavier than you look," I ground out.

The cat watched me unblinking. "Ten pounds of perfection."

"How long have you been staring at me while I slept, Hildo?"

The cat shrugged, his face still inches from mine. "I don't know. Maybe fifteen minutes? You've got an enormous nose hair protruding from your left nostril. I could pull it out if you want."

"I'm good. Thanks."

The first thing I'd done when I got home was to find the spell to bring Hildo back. He'd been right. It had been an easy spell, which involved the right incantation, one cat whisker (which I found in Iris's album Dana), and a few drops of my blood—and I had me a cat.

"Have you met my aunts?" I had neglected the part of warning them about our new friend. Mostly because I didn't want to wake them in the middle of the night. Besides, I really didn't think it would be a problem.

Hildo sat back on his haunches. "Yup. Ruth's already fed me two buttermilk pancakes."

I stared at the black cat, wondering how he could eat that much and where it all went.

"You snore when you sleep," commented the cat. "I was trying to figure out how such a small nose could produce a trumpet of horrors."

"Thanks."

"You're welcome." Hildo stepped over my face and let himself fall on my pillow behind my head, his tail whipping my forehead.

I shook my head. Cats. Kings of their domain, wherever they went. And apparently, familiars were no different.

I sat up and grabbed my phone. The clock said 11

a.m. "I have to take a shower." I jumped out of bed and practically ran to the mirror on my dresser. Yup. Still my thirty-year-old self.

"Why are you smiling like an idiot?" came the cat's drawl from my bed.

I turned on the shower. "Because it's Saturday. And Saturday's Marcus's day off."

"Who the hell is Marcus?"

I laughed and jumped in the shower. I closed my eyes and moaned at the hot water hitting my face, washing away all the last weeks' horrors. It was like I had peeled off my old skin and had come out a new, younger woman.

I felt a draft of cold on my back. I spun around and screamed.

"Hey! What are you doing? I'm naked here," I cried, trying to cover myself.

Hildo sat on the tile ledge of the shower, holding the shower curtain open with his paw.

The cat rolled his eyes. "Please. It's nothing that I haven't seen before." He peered inside. "Everything seems to be in the right place."

"Out!" I yanked the shower curtain back. "Don't make me regret bringing you back."

"Okay, okay, I get it," said the cat. "So, who's Marcus? Is he your boyfriend?"

I thought about it as I shampooed my hair.

"Maybe." Was he? I wasn't sure yet, but I was leaning toward a yes.

"You're going to go have sex with him. Aren't you?"

I frowned. "So, this is how it's going to be from now on. Right? You interrogating me about my personal life while I'm in the shower?"

"As your familiar, it's my business to know everything about you."

That was a little annoying, but the cat was too cute to be angry with, and I knew he was just trying to settle in as a familiar. Plus, nothing was going to ruin my mood today. Nothing.

After my shower, I brushed my teeth, put on my sexiest pair of undies and matching bra, pulled on my skinny jeans, matched them with a black top, and rushed down the stairs to the entryway.

Though I could smell Ruth's cooking, I wasn't even hungry.

Pulling on my boots, I peered into the kitchen. I could make out my aunts sitting at the kitchen table, but they weren't talking. Their faces were lined with worry. Something was off about how they were all sitting. It was as though their bodies were here physically, but their minds were elsewhere.

"They got a letter this morning," said the black cat who'd appeared at my feet, seemingly having spotted my concern.

I was about to ask what letter, but then I changed my mind. "I'll see you later," I told the cat. "Be good."

Hildo showed me his teeth in what I believed was his attempt at a wide grin. "I'm always good."

Right. I didn't believe that. I spun around. Before grabbing the door handle, I reached out and touched Gran's cane, which was leaning against the wall in the foyer where I'd left it last night. It had been good to me.

With my heart thrashing, I pulled open the door and ran out. I hit the street at a sprint, enjoying the feel of my legs pumping without the cacophony of bones grinding and knees popping.

The sun shone over my head, and most of the snow was melting, making the sidewalks wet and slippery.

I was grinning like an idiot. I knew it. And the few people I passed told me so with their bewildering expressions, seeing a smiling woman running down the street. I looked crazy. I felt crazy.

I barely even noticed the tall blonde with the body of a sports model. But when her face turned towards me, I halted.

"Holy shit, Allison." I tried to keep a straight face, but my facial muscles seemed to have a mind of their own. "What did you do to your eyebrows?"

Her perfectly manicured eyebrows were gone.

Like disappeared. Like someone had spelled them away...

Oh, dear.

Allison sighed dramatically, but without eyebrows, she looked like a robot. "What's this now?" She pressed her hands to her hips. "I'm not going to fall for any of your tricks. Not anymore. I've got a witch on my side now. I'm protected."

I made a face. "Ask for a refund."

I didn't know what she saw on my face that changed her mind, but she whirled her purse around, shoved her hand inside, and pulled out a mirrored compact.

She flipped it open...

Wait for it...

"Oh, my God! My eyebrows! My eyebrows are gone!" she howled, in a truly impressive voice.

"That's what I've been trying to tell you."

The gorgeous blonde's blue eyes rounded and ballooned like they might pop. She pressed her hands to her forehead in an attempt to hide what was already missing.

I kinda felt sorry for her.

Not really.

"You bitch!" she spat, and spittle flew from her mouth. "You did this to me." Then her expression turned truly ugly. "You're going to pay for this. I swear it! You're going to pay."

"Whatever." Like I said, nothing would get in the way of my good mood.

"Oh, don't worry, hon. I can draw you on some eyebrows." A plump woman in her early sixties marched our way, apparently having seen and heard the exchange. Her long, flowing wool coat of loud patterns in a mix of pink and black fluttered around her as she neared.

"Hi, Martha."

The witch glared at me, her bejeweled glasses sliding down her small nose. She turned to Allison and said, "And I have a hair growth serum spell that will grow them back in no time." She wrapped an arm around Allison's sobbing shoulders and pulled her away, but not before giving me an angry, disapproving scowl.

I shook my head, biting my lip so I'd stop smiling, but I couldn't. "Iris. You little devil."

I loved that Dark witch. Only a true friend would remove the eyebrows of your nemesis.

Smiling like it was my birthday again, I sprinted down the street, hit Marcus's building, yanked open the side door, and rushed to the top of the stairs.

I hit the platform a little out of breath and knocked.

Marcus pulled open the door. His gray eyes widened, and that damn near perfect mouth of his opened in shock. His reaction was even better than I had imagined.

The chief's face had more lines than I remember him having, his gray eyes accentuated by the dark circles under them. He'd clearly been worried and hadn't slept, but I was going to take care of that.

"Can I come in?" I brushed past him.

"Ah. Sorry, come in. Come in." He blinked a few times. "Tessa, you look—"

I raised a hand. "Hang on. And watch closely." I pulled off my jeans and black top. "Look," I said, beaming and hooking thumbs at myself.

Okay, so I did sound a little mad. But having been an eighty-year-old woman yesterday and now turning back into a thirty-year-old would make anyone a little mad.

A smirk came over him. His eyes shone and he laughed. "I'm looking."

"It's me. I'm me again." My body was nowhere near Allison's, not even close. I still had cellulite, my butt was a little saggier than I wanted, and I still had my batwings swaying under my arms. But it was me.

"You were always you," said the chief, his voice deep and filled with such desire that it left me breathless. "You were always beautiful."

Okie Dokie. "You owe me a birthday dinner, birthday dessert, birthday special, the whole shebang."

"The whole shebang," he purred. Then, in one swift movement, he managed to pull off his jeans, shirt, even his socks in a blink of an eye. Not really fair, when I thought about all the years of practice he'd had over me, being a wereape and having to get out of his clothes in under a few seconds to shift.

He stood there in all his half-naked glory, wearing only a grin and a tented pair of black boxers.

"Not bad," I teased, pulling my eyes away from his manhood. "But… can you do this—"

With a hard yank, I tried to pull off my sexy underwear but managed only to give myself a wedgie.

Marcus laughed. "Let me help you with that."

I wasn't going to argue.

He slipped his rough hands around the edge of my underwear, and my skin tingled where his fingers touched my hip. With a flick of his wrist, he pulled on the fabric and they tore apart. He dropped them on the floor and pressed against me.

Almost panting, I leaned into him, heat pounding in my core. He covered my mouth with his and a moan escaped me. His lips were demanding, aggressive. My mouth parted, and his tongue found mine. He let out a growl, his hold tightening around me. His rough but gentle hand slipped up to find my breast and I shuddered. Waves of desire rose high, almost frantic with need. I wanted him. All of him.

With a quick motion, he reached down, grabbed my ass, and lifted me up. Grinning savagely, I wrapped my legs around his waist.

"It's time for your dessert," he said breathily as he carried me to his bedroom.

29

"I'm home," I called as I pulled off my boots and tossed them in the entryway.

I hadn't wanted to leave Marcus, naked and alone, but I couldn't shut off this nagging feeling I had about my aunts. Something was up. And I wanted to know what that was.

Besides, I promised I'd come over again later tonight... for a *second* round.

We had spent the entire day in bed, watching movies and eating popcorn and junk food—mainly Twizzlers and grilled cheese. It had been one of the most enjoyable times of my adult life as we reminisced about our childhoods and laughed at each other's memories. I came to realize I enjoyed this man for much more than just his body.

Don't get me wrong, the sex was insanely good. But sharing his company like that was... even better.

I was beginning to see something real and profound developing between us—a rare something. Hopefully something we could build together that would last. And of course, it scared the crap out of me. It also forced me to face the harshest truth. If something should ever happen to the relationship, to us, it would hurt like hell. But it was worth it.

My phone vibrated and I pulled it out of my pocket and unlocked the screen, seeing a new text from Iris.

Iris: *I couldn't resist. Happy belated birthday.*

I texted back.

You're nuts.

Allison would not forgive me for the removal of her eyebrows. Or for the acne. If she did have a witch in her service, she would retaliate. It was going to get really ugly, really soon.

I didn't care.

Allison could have been more mature about my relationship with Marcus. The right thing to do was to accept that Marcus had moved on and then move on herself. We could have avoided all this ugliness, saved each other (her mostly) some hexes and curses. Maybe we could have been friends? Yeah, not really. Still, Allison had chosen to be a world-class bitch, trying to steal him from me and acting like a past jealous and disgruntled lover.

But when she has to fight a gorilla Barbie off of her man, a girl has to get a little dirty sometimes. Am I right?

I was just about to put my phone away when another text arrived. It was from Marcus.

Marcus: *Sorry about your undies.*

Me: *I'm not.*

Marcus: *Hurry back. I miss you.*

Smiling, I stuffed my phone in my pocket and headed for the kitchen. It was unusually quiet. The typical clatter of pots, murmurs of conversation, and the smells of dinner was nonexistent.

A black cat padded my direction down the hallway. His yellow eyes were bright, his long tail straight up behind him. "You've been gone a long time."

"I had things to do." Many, many things, and many, many times over.

Hildo halted and blinked up his yellow eyes at me, flicking his tail back and forth. "You smell like sex."

My face flamed. I lifted my arm and sniffed my armpit. "I don't know why I just did that."

The cat met my gaze steadily. "You had *relations* with this Marcus guy, eh? I have to meet him. Sooner rather than later."

I raised a brow as I stared at the black cat. "You *have* to meet him?"

"I'm your familiar," remarked Hildo, as though that gave him clearance to anything in my personal life, made him privy to all my secrets. "I have to meet all the guys you sleep with. It's a matter of safety. It's my duty to check them out. Make sure there's nothing untoward about them. You could be bumping uglies with the next Jack the Ripper for all we know."

I made a face. "I don't sleep with *guys*," I said, feeling the need to clear up that misinformation. "Just the one guy."

The cat shrugged and started to lick his front paw. "I still have to meet him," he mewed, his words muffled as he cleaned himself. "It's part of my job, to screen out the crazies."

I realized that he could be making this stuff up, since I had almost zero knowledge about familiars. And I had a feeling he knew this. Still, I found the idea of having Hildo watching my back comforting, though a little stalkerish, and I appreciated it.

I smiled. "You'll meet him. Soon," I added for good measure.

"Good," drawled the cat. "Now that we have that cleared, you better come quick."

"What's going on?" I frowned at his urgent tone.

"You'll see." Hildo ran back to the kitchen, leaving me to follow him.

When I entered the kitchen, my aunts were all still sitting around the kitchen table. None of them looked up as I approached, which I thought was strange. The fact that it looked like they hadn't even moved since this afternoon was even stranger.

What the hell was going on?

Crackers and cheese were laid out on the table, untouched. I pulled up a seat and sat, searching their faces. "Jesus. Who died?" I laughed as Hildo jumped up on my lap and began purring.

Finally, Beverly glanced over to me but then looked away. She was shaking her head in silence, emotions cascading over her pretty face in fear, anger, and dismay.

I moved my gaze over to Ruth. Her eyes were round, and she was rocking back and forth on her chair like a frightened bunny, ready to sprint.

Dolores was no better. Her long face was set in a grim concentration, her hands flattened on the table with a piece of paper in the middle. Could this be the letter Hildo had told me about?

They were clearly unhappy and freaked out about something.

"Why all the long faces?" I asked and stuffed a piece of cheese in my mouth. Hildo stared up at me expectantly, so I gave him one too.

"We need to tell you something, Tessa," stammered Ruth, looking frightened.

I swallowed my cheese. "Tell me what? Can't be that bad." I looked at their faces again. "Does it have something to do with that letter there?" I asked, eyeing the letter in front of Dolores.

Dolores let out a sigh. "It does."

I leaned forward, careful not to crush Hildo. "Well? Are you going to tell me, or do I have to make something up?"

"We," began Dolores, her voice tight. Her eyes moved from me to the letter. "We did something a long time ago."

"And now it's come back to bite us in the ass," finished Beverly as a wash of fear swept over her.

A drop of ice rolled from the back of my neck to my lower back. "What did you do?"

Dolores looked up at me and said, "We killed someone."

Well, crap.

Don't miss the next book in The Witches of Hollow Cove series!

BOOKS BY KIM RICHARDSON

THE WITCHES OF HOLLOW COVE

Shadow Witch

Midnight Spells

Charmed Nights

Magical Mojo

Practical Hexes

Wicked Ways

Witching Whispers

Mystic Madness

Rebel Magic

Cosmic Jinx

Brewing Crazy

WITCHES OF NEW YORK

The Starlight Witch

Game of Witches

Tales of a Witch

THE DARK FILES

Spells & Ashes

Charms & Demons

Hexes & Flames

Curses & Blood

SHADOW AND LIGHT

Dark Hunt

Dark Bound

Dark Rise

Dark Gift

Dark Curse

Dark Angel

ABOUT THE AUTHOR

Kim Richardson is a *USA Today* bestselling and award-winning author of urban fantasy, fantasy, and young adult books. She lives in the eastern part of Canada with her husband, two dogs, and a very old cat. Kim's books are available in print editions, and translations are available in over seven languages.

To learn more about the author, please visit:
    www.kimrichardsonbookstore.com

Printed in Great Britain
by Amazon